THE PRESIDENT IN HER TOWERS

ellipsis
• • •
press

THE PRESIDENT IN HER TOWERS

a report

TOM WHALEN

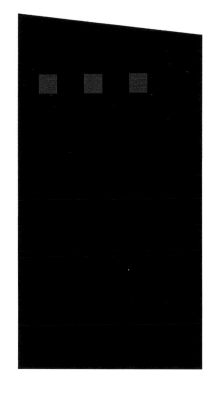

The President in Her Towers © 2012 Tom Whalen

Chapters of this novel in different form have appeared in *Caketrain, eye-rhyme, The Idaho Review, The Iowa Review, Keyhole, The Modern Review, Sonora Review, The Styles, Wordplay,* and in the chapbook *The Internecine Wars* (Obscure Publications).

Design by Corey Frost
Frontispiece: "Vogel-Selbsterkenntnis" (17th Century)

First Edition
ISBN 0-9637536-7-3
ISBN-13 978-0-9637536-7-0

Distributed to the trade by Small Press Distribution, Berkeley, California
Toll-free number (U.S. only): 800-869-7553
Bay area/International: 510-524-1668
orders@spdbooks.org
www.spdbooks.org

Ellipsis Press LLC
P.O. Box 721196
Jackson Heights, NY 11372
www.ellipsispress.com

OTHER BOOKS BY Tom Whalen

Elongated Figures

Winter Coat

Roithamer's Universe

Dolls: Prose Poems

The Birth of Death and Other Comedies:
The Novels of Russell H. Greenan

Steck sich ein ganß selbst bey Der Nasn
Waß dich nit Freudt Thue auch nicht Blasn

In Token
of My Gratitude for Her Support,
This Book is Inscribed
To
Heide Ziegler

At any rate, Acton, with his characteristic discretion, forebore to give expression to whatever else it might imply, and the narrator of these incidents is not obliged to be more definite.

Henry James, *The Europeans*

1. The President and Her Deans

The President laughs to herself at night deep in her cups. She laughs to herself in her office, at the podium that has special gadgets built into it for her alone, gadgets that allow her to monitor the wakefulness of the audience, one by one. In her refrigerator are seven bottles of Frascati. Each day her refrigerator is replenished without her even having to ask.

The President holds a conference on the Wings of Misery that are sweeping through the corridors of the University. She holds a conference on the feasibility of the Balloon Classroom and the Maintenance of the Mysterium. She holds a conference on conferences held in foreign capitals and wonders aloud if she should not travel to one or more of these foreign universities to enhance her knowledge of their inner workings. Her deans sway with her words like poplars in a November wind heralding the first hard snow.

The President fires her secretary, hires her again, fires her again, hires her again. Good secretaries are hard to come by, she notes in her presidential notebook.

The President is the first woman President at a university in her country. She takes note of this fact, but she bears it little importance. She is a bootstrap sort of woman. She got here on her own. She had no help from her colleagues. That is certainly the case. Her colleagues fear her. And well they should. She is, after all, the President. She ran on a platform of hope and retribution, and was elected by a wide margin, an astonishing one, in fact, though the second election was close, too close; she had to make some changes; she made them, and her betrayers were sorry. Still, dissent is healthy for any system.

Often she tests the system by announcing meetings at midnight. The deans come stumbling in in their nightclothes, their dressing gowns, their night caps. They are a motley group. There is (as best I can translate the German titles) the Dean of Why I Am Here, the Dean of Let Me Have It, the Dean of I Can't Take Any More, the Dean of Happenstance, the Dean of Neuroscience, the Dean of Petrography, the Dean of Muscle Tone, the Dean of Music, the Dean of the Sonnet and the Villanelle, the Dean of the Sestina, the Dean of Pessimism Overrun by Lapidary Meliorists, the Dean of Religion, the Dean of Pertinacity (who always wears a peruke, as stated in the by-laws of the University), the Dean of Pests and Pester, the Dean of Oh Lord What Are We To Do Now That Our Rope Has Ended, the Dean of Fear and Trembling and his sister dean the Dean of Leaping, the Dean of Recalcitrance, the Dean of Worship, the Dean of Dreams (who never shows up; the President would fire him if she could locate his office), the Dean of the The (my favorite—his firm handshake, his friendly welcome), The Dean of I Can't Go On, the Dean of Opposites, the Dean of Students (an old dean who hasn't met with a student in years), the Dean of Holidays, the Dean of Zoos, the Dean of Mercurial Talents—about whom the President asks me to file a brief report:

The Dean of Mercurial Talents said: I have become a commodified artefact. A thought comes to me and immediately it is raised into the air like a trial balloon, and for a moment everyone is interested, what will it bring, what will it mean, but then everyone is as suddenly disinterested in the trial balloon, the sky after all is filled with trial balloons, why should we be interested in this one rather than another, and so it goes with the balloons I raise off the surface of my bald dome.

After watching the restored *Metropolis*, the Dean shouted: It's all been a shadow play! The lights in the projection booth shut down. Boys and girls in white shirts with red vests toss fallen popcorn and candy wrappers into yellow plastic bags. Outside the cinema the Dean saw in the green sky a biplane and a zeppelin. Seagulls lifted off from the parking lot as he made his way toward the Mystic Mall.

The President likes my report. She likes my panache. I am flattered, but I am also wary. Always be wary and you will never be weary, my grandmother said. I don't know what she meant, but because she was so much older than I, I always believed my

9

grandmother, memorized her every saying, of which she had many. I was raised on wild plum jelly and apple pies. I was raised to be a good boy, obedient, but not too obedient. To hell with them if they can't take a joke, my grandmother said. In her nineties she wrote a novel that became a bestseller. It was called *The Secret Sex Life of a Great-Grandmother*. It sold in the thousands. It was a fantastic success in her home state of Arkansas. She was a cause célèbre among feminists.

Is this, I wonder, why the President hired me?

2. Why I Was Hired

Sometimes when I consider why the President (her proper title is Ihre Magnifizenz, but since I know her personally, albeit not intimately, I may refer to her as the President), why, as I was saying, she hired me as her personal assistant, it all seems a dream or the dream of a madman, as if somehow I had slipped through the loop of narrative time like a minnow through a sieve, and now imagine myself a young man at work at Chet Darling's Downtown Mobil with Pegasus caught in mid-flight above the lube bay doors and me at rest on a wooden Coca-Cola rack, in my grease-stained t-shirt and jeans, an oily red rag used for cleaning dip sticks dangling out of my back pocket like a strange tail, me caught in a pump jockey's dream of better things, a copy of *The Princess Casamassima* in one hand and Wellek and Warren's *The Theory of Literature* in the other (which shouldn't date me so much as tell you what education was like for a young Arkansas lad with a M.A. degree once upon a time, and for all I know may still be, nor should it cast a negative or autumnal light on either of the two books mentioned whose value, like so much of true worth, transcends time), dreaming of a life elsewhere, somewhere other than where I am, though where I am is not all to my disliking, what with Pegasus' hooves right over me and the ice house still to clean, huge blocks of ice to wash down and grapple with on a hot summer day, nothing like it, nothing like it in this world, there at Chet Darling's Downtown Mobil Station, adream on the wooden Coca-Cola rack..., when suddenly the bell-rope bangs me awake and a black limousine pulls in, a window rolls down and a woman (Ihre Magnifizenz) leans her head out the window and, with only a trace of an accent, tells me she is the rector of a university in a country across the ocean and she is on a search for a new personal assistant, her old personal assistant having committed errors which she would not like at the moment to go into, but later, yes, later she would be glad to tell me about them, if I were willing to listen to them, if I were willing (here, she pauses and smiles that smile that is her mark of... what? character? authority? mystery?) to become her personal assistant. And I say yes.

I said yes yes yes, but that was not at all how it went, how I was hired, how I was hired was not at all like what I just fantasized. But I am prone to fantasy (as a doctor once told me), and how it was I came to be hired as the President's personal assistant I have in the end no answer. Indeed, I attribute it most days to an act of magic. But by whom? The President herself? This possibility I do not dismiss. My being hired might as well be attributed to divine intervention. I do not in any way consider myself worthy of such an intervention, but the President..., yes, the President I can imagine commanding the attention of the gods. What I can with absolute certainty say is that the universe contains much more matter than we have yet been able to identify and that this matter might partake of enough magic and mystery and divinity to answer the questions mankind has been asking all these years, and among the questions that could surely be answered would be how I came to be placed as the personal assistant to the President of the University. Stranger things surely can be imagined and have been.

Once I dreamed I was on a bicycle and the President was also on a bicycle (such an occurrence could never happen in real life, such a thing is unimaginable except in dreams, and I would never never tell this dream or any of my dreams to the President, nor would she care a fig for my or anyone else's dream, so much rubbish, so much tripe, so much likely kitsch— I see her shudder at the thought, see her cringe at the cliché most dreams must inevitably be) and I turned to her and asked her why she had hired me (I would never ask her that in real life) and she said (in my dream), *Épater le bourgeois.*

But enough of dreams and my silly musings. What is important about the President is her *presence* and her *will to action.* I have seen her when she was alone in her office, a glass of Frascati in her hand, resisting the forces of her many enemies through her will alone, her back rigid, her lips tight, but a flicker of a smile playing across them, and with each flicker I could imagine a problem solved, an enemy felled, a building raised toward the city's skies, workers and

students and administrators already filling this building, scrambling along its top floors even before the
ground had been broken. This is the President I know
well, the President whom I work for, whose wishes I
obey to the best of my abilities, knowing all along full
well that they are not enough, but that if I could do
better I would, and if I encountered someone whom I
thought could do my job more efficiently and imagi-
natively I would gladly, as a matter of duty, tender
my resignation and suggest her or him as my replace-
ment. However I don't think it would ever be a she,
even though about the President there floats an aura
of the *Ewig-Weibliche*, the Eternal Feminine, as if all
that womankind had ever been or ever will be had
found a home in her bearing.

Perhaps I am speaking *ex mero motu*, but for
that I can be forgiven; it's difficult to keep one's feel-
ings in check regarding the President, whether one
admires her (as do I) or hates her (as do her many
enemies). When she walks down the hall, trailed or
not by an entourage, one knows that she and only she
is the President. And yet she possesses a humility that
makes her seem almost vulnerable; you want to come
to her aid, do what you can for her and at your own
expense. This I consider the true sign of power, of authority. We (those of us on her side) will lay down
our dinner forks, our cups of coffee, our newspapers
and paperbacks and student essays and rush to her
aid at her command. If she asks me to meet her at
midnight at the König X, I will be there, pen in one
hand, notebook in the other. If she asks me to meet
the reporters from Johannesburg at the airport and

show them the city, I will be there with a guide map and hotel reservation for each of them. If she asks me to write her a speech for two weeks hence, I will deliver it within two days, because she might want to look over what I have written and ask me to rewrite it or revise it herself.

But here I must be careful. Slavish obedience is not what she is after. Is that why her former personal assistant was humiliated out of his position? She hasn't told me that story yet, but hints abound. He was seen consorting with the enemy. His reports were too dry. He could not take criticism. Little things (the Frascati, for example) were not attended to with alacrity. He obeyed her all too well. He could not foresee soon enough her troubled moods. Hints and rumors.

Yesterday she fired the Dean of Weather, the Provost of Storms.

I must be careful.

3. The German Student Today

    The President asks me to file a report on the German Student Today, and I write:

    The German student today more often than not lives in a basement or attic, from which he or she can see a gray sky, mostly gray, generally gray shading into a grayer gray, like slate upon which nothing is written. The lights of the city, if she lives in the attic, sparkle beneath her like a country she will never enter, a country about which she can only dream. For the German student does not know a fig about how the city works, about how the dynamos of civilization funnel their energies into keeping the city lights lit, the two Towers of the University humming in space in order for the German student today to learn about the nature of the universe or the system that maintains him there in his attic or basement, but as oral exams have shown never learns, or never learns in that completeness and fullness that would make her professors say, Ah, yes, our student, one of ours, see how she has learned all that we wished her to learn, how she makes her way into the wide world trailing our imparted knowledge like a cloak across the wide field, yes, yes. No, this the professors never say; they are dissatisfied; they have, rightly, high expectations for their pupils, standards so high they can never be met, which is as it should be. Dissatisfaction is the sister of the establishment, accomplishment its grandmother. We are young, but we are also old, the professors say to themselves when the German student today visits them in their ficus-filled offices. The German student today does not often visit these offices, I am sorry I have to report (though rumors about one Herr Dunkelbach abound). The German student today prefers never to step into these offices for reasons that do not bear significantly on this report. What is it that the German student today prefers to do? She prefers to stare out her windows upon the gray sky, whether it is snowing or not, always a gray sky, a gray cloud rises above the Towers of the University, one above the Humanities Tower and another above the Sciences Tower. The German student today prefers not to study the composition of this gray cloud, she prefers to simply stare out the window of her attic room and dream of being somewhere else. Books line the room of the student, books that are required reading at the University, but in truth these books are more often than not written in a language comprehensible to no one but the initiated, and the German student to-day has yet to be initiated into the language of these books. Herein lies a fault or divide or great abyss of the system, but alas the German student today appears unwilling even to attempt a crossing of this abyss, or to take a leap over or into it. The German student today dreams, if he is male, of a music that he has never heard before, a music that will serve as a key into the higher spheres, without his first having to work his way up through the system, as his professors and the President have done. And if she is female, then the German student today dreams of dying in the arms of a cloud in the shape of a minotaur. On the survey "The German Student Today and the Problems of the University" 79% of the students responded in the affirmative to the question "Does the theory of ex-matriculation mean more to you than the ex-matriculation itself?" In the same survey 82% of the students could distinguish an airplane from a balloon (up 12% from the previous two decades). Suicides and abortions have risen in tandem, but no correlation between the two has yet been established, although the Dean of Theology and Food Services believes it's only a matter of time that a significant relationship is confirmed. The Dean of Biomechanics promises an addendum to this report in which he will suggest a week in Zürich to see how students there compare with ours and what measures need be taken in order for our students to rise above the Swiss. The Dean of

Biomechanics is sure he has the means to achieve success beyond the President's wishes. I personally do not trust the Dean of Biomechanics. He is an untrustworthy fellow and possibly dangerous. He is *in potentia* if not in fact an enemy of the President. He has asked me to state in this report that he is not to be trifled with and that he adores the President as much as anyone, as much as Petrography does or Weather did. 100% of the German students today could identify the President by name, give her proper title, and state the names of at least three of her books, the most frequently cited titles being *Unnötige Ironie, oder die schöne Deutschen* (*Unnecessary Irony, or the Beautiful Germans*) and *Unmenschlichkeit und die ganze Universität* (*Inhumanity and the Whole University*). The German student today desires most of all a clarification of the requirements toward ex-matriculation. These requirements are in the process of being rewritten. The students wonder if they will ever ex-matriculate. Many of the students have no idea what life outside the University and their attic or basement apartments is about. They stare at the revolving Daimler-Benz sign above the Hauptbahnhof, as do I, late into the night, wondering what life is all about. What does it mean to be a student? Is this the right path to follow, the path of academe? What exactly is life? Are the Towers more about their past, their present, or their future? These thoughts roam the hallways and corridors and basements and attics of the minds of

19

the German students today. The lights of the city are blue and green and red and yellow, and this the students appreciate. Is it possible, they wonder, for them, if only once, to peer into the chamber of the Sleeping or Dead Deans? The German student today does not wish to make this a formal request. The German student today is neither entirely content nor discontent, a not altogether inaccurate indication of his character. They wish their wishes or even their words were more attended to, but they do not want to complain. They are students, they know above all that they are only students. They dream, these young men and women, the German students today, when they dream at all, most often of making love to their stepsisters.

The President looks up from reading my report. Is that the flicker of a smile I see on her lips? I cannot say, but I am not worried. It is she who must decide whether or not a response written or verbal is necessary. She merely nods and motions for me to bring her a Frascati, but I know she is thinking about what I have written and whatever action she takes will bear more meaning than I, her assistant, could ever possibly fathom.

4. The Gypsy Problem

The Gypsy Problem!

Yes, the gypsy problem was upon us during my first week with the President. And here I learned how she could solve the seemingly unsolvable.

Thirty gypsies were living in the Humanities Tower. Thirty gypsies! Their abiding in the building went against all the laws of the University. No one was allowed to stay in either the Humanities Tower or the Sciences Tower past nine at night, except professors up late working on their experiments (e.g. wave functions and in-flame diagnostics) or course preparations (e.g. Malfeasance and Memory, or Monopolated Mysteries of the Mid-Fifteenth Century). But the student council had allowed a gypsy and her two children to stay in the student council room during the night, after all the students had gone to their apartments or the apartments of their parents or their parents' parents, and now the three gypsies had multiplied by ten—thirty gypsies were staying in the student council room.

Who but the President would have thought of her solution?

The faculty senate raged. They wanted to call in the retired deans, they wanted to call in the police, the fire department, historians, storm watchers, death troops, even though the latter had been officially banned decades ago. They wanted the President to bite the bullet and force the gypsies' hand; they wanted her to say, We must burn the gypsies out! They wanted her to give way, to step aside, to abdicate, retire. They wanted her to think, Yes, I am the President, but I cannot be President forever, someday I must give up my authority, I must allow for new elections as stated in by-law 3342 as amended by me in the midnight of my first term to allow for the indefinite postponement of new elections. I have been here too long. One's perception changes, gridlines form and shift under one's feet and suddenly where one thinks one is, one isn't. Yes, I must give up. I must give up. *Gib's auf! Gib's auf!* Give it up, give it up! rings throughout the faculty senate. *Gib's auf! Gib's auf!*

Would the Gypsy Problem be the answer her enemies had been waiting for? Now was the time for them to strike. When she was weak. When she could not handle what was surely the crisis of the year for the University. Yes, now was the time for her to resign, to back down, say that the time had come for her to relinquish her power to the council itself. She had served too long. The Gypsies were beyond her. Yes, I will have no more truck with authority. No more posing atop the ladder of power, when certainly I do not belong there. I humbly resign. That's what she should say. That's what her enemies wanted to hear. The gypsies must go, the senate shouted. *Gib's auf! Gib's auf!*

How poorly they knew their leader!

Dear Herr Gehülfe, my little assistant, my little flower, she said to me. Come see what your President can do.

And she rose from her black office chair, rose in the elevator to the top of the Tower and took me by the hand, as the wind whipped off the surrounding mountains, whipped the birches and beech trees as if they were hair on a dark maiden. Elsters and crows curved across the gray sky. Was it S Tower itself that I felt moving beneath my feet, or only a weakness in my knees? Was it my fear of heights that made me tremble, or my awe at her aura of command?

Beneath us the gypsies hovered out of the cold in their one room in H Tower. Could she turn them out in the dead of winter? Into the snow? Herd them herself back into the mountains?

I myself had only seen the gypsies once. I was walking down the stairs carrying documents for the President from H Tower to S Tower when a child, I think three years old, raised his hand to mine, grasped it, and said, *Komm*. I walked him down the stairs where at the bottom two young girls in colorful clothing took him from me and disappeared into the basement. At the time I thought they were the children of one of the custodians, but now I know they were gypsies illegally residing in the University.

Standing beside the President atop the Tower, I felt no larger than the gypsy child who had taken my hand, and I cowered as she bent down to me and whispered in my ear, What you are about to see you must never never never tell anyone, must never write in your diary, must never telephone back home to the States, must in effect erase from your memory. In fact, what memory of it you will have will not be memory but dream, a dream dreamed by a dreamed dreamer. Do you understand?

I nodded, and then from her head sprouted a feather, her coat spread its wings, her eyes narrowed, the cold reddened her cheeks, and from her head now grew a long neck, the neck of a goose, the neck of a swan, an anhinga. It grew and grew, it curved into the air, formed an exclamation mark, a question mark, an ampersand, and her feet were bird's feet, her feet were claws, the beak stretched around in the air, searching for food, searching for other birds, and the sky reddened, the sky rolled up like a newspaper, the clouds folded into themselves, and her arms disappeared into her sides.

Atop the Tower I swayed and fainted.

When I awoke we were in the air, the President and I. I was caught in one of her horny claws, and on her neck clung the thirty gypsies, one hand of each of them clutching her feathers, the other holding onto their luggage, paper bags, carpets, coats, phonographs, lamps and lampshades, and we were flying over the mountains.

The President turned her bird face to her real face and with her beak bit her nose. I am the bird of self knowledge, I am Vogel Selbsterkenntnis, she said. I will make the wind breathe for me. I will make the clouds bow down and kiss my forehead. Her bird's beak pecked at her feathers.

The mountains spread out beneath us like meringue on a pie, and I wanted to be anywhere but where I was. I didn't want to believe that we were flying over the snowy mountains. I wanted to be in my apartment, looking out onto the lights of the city. I wanted to be dreaming there of the President in her Towers, or of living elsewhere, or of Arkansas, or of nothing, and when I awoke from my reverie I wanted to see the white, blue-edged Mercedes-Benz insignia rotating high atop the Hauptbahnhof.

But you are where you are, the President said, and whoever bites their nose, bites their own face. Where we are going, where I and my worthy assistant are taking you, is to a land where caravans travel of themselves over the mountains. Do you understand?

I did not, nor, I suppose, did the gypsies, whose faces were scarred and frozen with terror. I clung tight as I could to the huge breast of the bird and tucked my head into her feathers to protect myself from the ice wind.

Above me the gypsies squabbled and the sound of the bird's huge wings pounded against my ears, but still I could hear her speaking.

Anyone who can make their own nose grow, will always know which way the wind blows. Beyond that I cannot help you gypsies. The alternatives would have been, I assure you, much worse.

And then she shook herself, and we clutched her even harder, as her long neck wrapped round and round her head, until only a single eye peered out from beneath her feathers.

The eye blinked (winked?) at me, and I wanted to shout, Ihre Magnifizenz, spare me!, but then her claw let go, and I fell, fell, into a darkness thicker than dream...

When the senate reconvened the next morning, the President said, I've taken care of the Gypsy Problem.

5. A Conference on Snow

The winds in the Towers. They come, they go, like the President herself. I sit in my small, white cubicle staring out at the snow that blankets the sidewalk between H Tower and S Tower and fills the air with its heavy flakes, and for days I do not see the President.

I do not know her itinerary; that is, I know only those parts of it she wants me to know. In the ninth floor cubicle, I look out the window at the snow-capped highrises of the city, at the radio tower on the Raichberg, at the clouds that spread over the sky like a hand, like the hand of the President over my forehead one day when I said I had a fever.

I think I'm a little ill, I said, a little woozy. The world trembles in its veins, I said. I'm not at all sure that I am what one might call entirely well, I might indeed be a little sick, a little not altogether well, I said. I believe I'm sick, *ich habe etwas Kopfweh*, a little trembling in those regions of thought where there should be none.

She placed her hand on my hot forehead, and the fever retreated like a wave from shore. Without saying a word, the President turned and left my cubicle.

Alone in my cubicle for days on end, no secretary, no deans, no custodians ever come here unless the President especially requests it. Mostly I stare out the window and await spring, and in spring I assume I will await winter; each season has its own music, its own ministries, but what I need is seldom found in the season at hand. When I am not busy staring out the window or writing a speech or preparing a report, I stack the papers that litter the shelves of my cubicle. These papers are filled with notes by the President and I have been told to catalogue them, but the task is so daunting (her script is the old German Sutterlin script that neither I nor her peers can decipher) that I usually shuffle the pages from one stack marked "Miscellaneous" to another marked "Misc." to another marked "File Under ?"

Where the winds come from, I do not know. The windows are double-paned, the doors sealed tight. But still I feel a wind, the papers on my desk ripple under my gaze, the words shimmer and fade, a leaf falls to the floor. I pick it up, wonder which stack it came from, place it on the one nearest at hand, and consider the problem of the winds. I have not asked the President about them, fearful that she would think me naive or overly inquisitive. And I am sure that somewhere in the University a professor and his assistants are busy at work on the calculus needed to explain the winds' origins, their velocity, their telemetry and teleology.

Then the door opens and the President is standing there, the President whom I haven't seen in days,

there in her conservative dress, her white blouse buttoned up to the neck, her dark brown hair cut more
long than short, her suit black, her skirt long, her
black, tiny (for such a handsome woman) patent
leather shoes snug on her feet.

Are you ready? she asks, and I shuffle my papers
into a stack, place on it the clear glass paperweight
with a snow-filled Swiss landscape frozen inside it (a
gift from the President), and we are off to... where? A
conference, yes, it must be a conference. A conference
in the snow, the streets thick with it, the air swirling
up and down with it, the green houses white-capped,
the cedar limbs calling the snow down.

The new Dean of Weather is here and so is the
Assistant Dean of Snow, and the weather appears to
be to the President's liking. Around an oval table we
gather, I at a discreet distance from her side, the deans
at the other end of the table, far away. I can barely
make them out, and their words come to me in frag-
ments: music of the everything, the haunted air, the
sizeable will remain in the making of the loss that we
know to be in the night made up of the mystery of
antennae, nomenclatures remembered when not forgotten the many cities and requirements satellites in
the halls and the windows.

I write all this down, I write down everything,
because the President will later ask me to repeat it
back to her as she sits at her desk, the room dim, a
glass at her elbow. But for now I can only assume what
they say will make sense to her. Later, I think, the
President will understand that which I cannot.

She nods to me as if she has heard my thoughts,

29

and I see that her hair is only a little ruffled by the snow, her cheeks ruddy from the cold. The wind, I wonder, has it taken us here to this conference? And she nods again, and the conference begins in earnest.

I cannot see the deans any longer nor make out what they are saying. All around us the snow continues to fall. The table is covered, I cannot even see my notebook. It is lost somewhere between my eyes and knees. I wonder what I am to do, and I want to panic, but instead I smile up into the implacable face of the President who looks down upon me and nods once more and then whispers into my ear: This is winter we are in, my boy. Take it with you wherever you go. The wind is in the winter, the winter in the wind. We make our way to the doors of the churches, the classrooms, the Towers even in this weather. This is why we have winter. The music that you hear is not the falling of the snow but the ticking of the mice within the walls. They are waiting as I am waiting, waiting for our deans to stop mumbling into their beards, to stop their nonsense, their abuse of the students who know nothing, who will never know anything because they are students, they will never pass beyond this state of being into another. Why don't they understand this? Do they think the snow will stop falling because they wish it to?

The President pauses, and I hear the wind whistling in the crevices of my thoughts, then she continues, her voice lower, her voice no more than a whisper in a dream: When the weather turns to winter, when the snow falls like it is falling now, the deans cannot stop it. No one can. Not even I can stop the snow when the weather seizes us by the arms and tells us: now you must leave, now you must batten down the tarpaulin of your self, now you must make ready for the truth of the winter that knows only itself, is only itself, like a drum that beats without a drummer, and the northern sky opens up for your return. This is what the wind is telling us now, the wealth of snow fallen on your eyelids, the branches sagging from the weight of sleep. Can you hear me? Are you still here?

I raise my head from the pillow of my arms, stare out the window of my cubicle where the winds have blown me again. Outside it is snowing a thick snow that covers the Towers, the trees. I can barely make out the other Tower now and the faint figure of the President at her eleventh floor window in S Tower, alone in her office as I am alone in my cubicle in HT, and the snow thick between us, the winds quiet now, the papers on my desk calm, waiting for me to tend to them, waiting for this season to pass, for the snow to cease, for spring to return.

And then I can no longer see her, and then the Tower itself vanishes, and in the window I see only myself, and of myself there is little or nothing to say. What need I, I wonder, to think of myself when I am the assistant to the President?

So I lift the paperweight off the stack on my desk and begin again the business of cataloguing.

6. "Her Life"

I am to write a little biography of the President! Nothing too grand, she says, not a hagiography, just a simple story of her past, something for the petitioners to read who wait in the outer chambers of her office. Nothing too fantastic, she says and smiles at me, and I see on the tip of her front teeth a trace of her lipstick, which she, with an almost invisible touch of a finger, rubs off.

A biography! How can I complete such an assignment? My pencil lead breaks from the thought of the effort. The life of the President in five hundred words? *Quelle catastrophe!* A little tale to amuse the masses, she says. Simple, discreet, a touch of the fairy tale would not be unwelcome. *Es war einmal*, it might begin. She slides her left index finger along my cheek, taps playfully the tip of my nose, then exits.

But how am I to begin when there is so much I don't know, can never know, never begin to fathom about the President, this strange, altogether charming figurine of wit and wisdom far beyond my understanding? Her own peculiar ethical impulses that make her, for example, struggle against her administration's enemies instead of giving in to their mad whims, or simply going into exile—to the U.S. or China—these impulses, whatever they might be, I am unable to comprehend. I know only that I, on the deepest level, admire her, but this does me no good when it comes to composing a biography of the President. But begin I must, and begin I shall.

So I begin, somehow, I begin with her academic career, her struggle to overcome the prejudices of her professors, the disdain of her Herr Vater Doktor Professor who did not want to approve her dissertation *Unnötige Ironie, oder die schöne Deutschen* but who was forced to when the book was published and acclaimed by every newspaper and journal in the German Democratic Republic and translated into fifteen languages. But already this seems simultaneously implausible and too modest.

So I start again, this time beginning with an incident from her childhood which every professor under her now knows by heart, how when she was only six a balloon drifted over the roof of her parents' house while she was reading Apuleius on her windowsill, and when she looked up she saw the balloon and instinctively clutched its dangling rope and was lifted into the air, into the blue afternoon sky, a child of six, and she climbed the rope and dropped into the balloon's basket, where she found cheese and wine enough to sustain her as the balloon drifted into the Alps, finally to come down in Altsdorf four days later, where reporters awaited her with their notepads and cameras, and she told a tale of how a giant had taken her away into the region of the ice mountains and wanted her to misbehave, but her parents (who died of shock when they discovered her absence) had taught her how to handle giants, and she felled him with one stroke of an axe and took off again in her balloon, and met other monsters, other demons, whom she dispatched with equal alacrity.

But how drab this fairy tale seems in comparison to the President I know (and who knows her better than I?), how mundane, how commonplace. No, I think, I cannot do it. I cannot begin to express, no matter how simple my approach, the complexity of the President.

If I were an artist I could capture, perhaps, with a brushstroke, the mixture of regality and compassion, the smallness that radiates an immense magnitude, the elegance of her hand as it lays down her pen, the grayness of her eyes that shade into blue the deeper you look into them, and the blue into a deeper blue, and the dark blue into blackness from which you expect something to arise like smoke from its depths. But I am no artist, am hardly even a writer. I can file reports, write speeches on Thanksgiving when the President has to appear at a dinner for those students who have flown from my country to study at the University. But a narrative of the President's life in five hundred words? *C'est impossible!*

But the impossible is exactly what she expects from her staff, and I sit at my desk, look out upon the other Tower where she at this moment sits in her office awaiting my report or tending to matters that

I am not privy to, matters that do not concern her personal assistant, matters that are for the President alone, and I write:

HER LIFE

She was born in Small Village at the foot of the Great Mountains; her mother died in an avalanche, her father in the War. Orphaned at four she made her way through life and at the age of sixteen knitted twelve thousand red sweaters. She does not request preferential treatment, nor does she give the same. In all matters she behaves honestly. Her pride is not a sin, but the remains of her sorrow at the loss of all that she wished to accomplish and now knows, from the perspective of maturity and wisdom, cannot be accomplished in one lifetime. She is as modern as she need be, and as traditional as the day is long. She cares most about her deans, her students, her staff, but her warmth is general all over the country. Politics is her wardrobe, she says, education her bread. After Fastnacht, she fasts for three weeks. During this time the Hugo Mountains welcome her, and again for three weeks in the summer she goes into retreat in these valleys. A wise old man of the mountains sees to it that she has quiet, that she has time to meditate and food to eat. Late afternoon in the park, with the sunlight laying its golden cloak over the snow, I have seen red squirrels feed out of her hand. Each morning when her staff

convenes around her, she says, "It's only a beginning always," and reinvigorated by these words
we go about our business. I imagine her alone
in her Towers, alone in her apartment up on the
hill overlooking the city, alone with her authority, chilled by it, but chilled like a bottle of good
wine is chilled before one sits down to a dish of
Swabian *Maultaschen*, pasta stuffed with meat,
in a restaurant on Urbanstrasse. When she walks
home, the leaves in the trees shiver with music as
she passes. Her favorite dish: Plum Pudding. Her
favorite book: Grimmelshausen's *The Adventures
of Simplicius Simplicissimus*. In the city's muse-
um hangs a painting of her called *Die schwank-
ende Frau* (The Hesitant Woman). The moon
looks in through her window, just as it does on
anyone who has a penthouse with west-facing
windows. The Gestation Chamber was her idea,
no one else's, despite the rumors to the contrary,
no one else's but hers. Initiatives from the office
of the President have caused the University to
increase its efficiency rate by 63%. Should the
time come when the President is no longer the
President, the University shall go into a volun-
tary mourning of eighty-two days and six hours.
The mystery of the winds, of the Towers, of the
cellar of the sleeping or dead deans can be solved
under her administration. I have not forgotten
how much I owe her my job, my life, my soul.
A new-found rhythm pulses through the halls
of the University. At the moment four publish-
ers are vying for the rights to her life. Sightings

of angels have increased by 99%. What is the Great Sickness if not the smoke from the stacks on the horizon that the President will, if granted a long enough tenure, clean up. The President at the moment is in her office. She promises to improve matters. Matters, she says, will improve. Her life so far has been full and rewarding. Her future promises even more of the same. She has no brothers or sisters. All gifts to the President must, by law, be donated to charity. Courage, she says, is the Mother of Invention; Mystery, she says, the Great Motivator.

The angels, she tells me, when I show her my copy, yes, I like the angels, and orders a print run of a hundred thousand copies.

7. Rumors (I)

Rumors in the hallways. I have heard them fluttering in and out of the niches in the walls. They say the President's position is in jeopardy; they say she won't last; they say that someone from Earth Sciences is going to discover a new underground bridge to the heart of the President's power and then blow it up. Rumors, phantasmagoric but possibly true, and I feel obliged to report them. If only I can wend my way through the maze that takes one to her office. Is she on the ninth floor today of this Tower, or the eleventh of S Tower? Like a child who has lost his bearings, I enter a door, enter another. Will she listen to me? Will she recognize the seriousness of her position? Her hair, pulled tight around her head like a helmet, does not move when she rises from her chair.

Food, she says, we must think more about the uses of food. Does it matter that, my dear assistant, we eat each and every day? Why not begin the week with a fast, a prayer to the gods, an embracing of absence and abstinence? We are not birds, Herr Thomas, we need not grub for our worms. The air, Thomas, the air must be our food. We breathe life into us, and we release it out again. Consumption is not the answer; forgoing is. Shall I do that, my boy, shall I appoint a Dean of Forgoing?

Her voice is light, indifferent to the urgency of my report, willing to discourse on appetites versus necessity, but beneath it I hear a mountain wanting to awake, a forest seizing up in the winter cold, ice snapping the branches. The room darkens around us. The world is a distant place when I am with the President in her chambers. I cannot say for sure but I think that a storm has settled over the city. Do the Towers create the weather or vice-versa? Her voice continues, I hear what I hear, above, below...

The President asks me to sit down, sit down, my dear assistant, you are weary from these rumors. They terrify you, but they need not. I am thinking about them even when I discourse on the fare at the Mensa, even when I say that on Tuesdays they must never serve potato pizza, they must not put bread sticks ever again in the greasy soup. We must think beyond the oil, beyond the vinegar. A life awaits the students, even though they think it does not, when they leave or are dismissed or ex-matriculate from the University. But here, dear Thomas, among those of us who work for the University, no matter in what capacity, no one grows if they cannot rise above the tide of rumors that sweep through the corridors and hallways and attic spaces, basement depths, of the University. Yes, I know they believe I have had unsavory connections to the Minister of Mysterium. Think on what you have heard, don't think on it, let it drift into the next room and then let that room drift into the next and the next into the next. Are you where you once were? No one can answer the riddle of the Towers. They are talking about me, yes, yes, I know it. They want me to leave, to hang up my robes, my cloak, my adornments. But what are these things? Nothing of value. I need them not. Rumors of war? Of course, there are wars going on all around us, Thomas, if you would but look for them. File a report, file another report. What are you here for if not to file reports? This is a lesson you are to learn, but no one can teach it to you. That I learned a long time ago. No one can teach you or me or the students anything. They can learn, but learn they must on their own. We cannot help them, no more than you can stop the rumors that are swirling, gathering force around us. They are coming, yes, my dear assistant, something is coming, and I cannot stop it. But I can meet it. And this is what they fear, that I can meet what is coming with an indifference that will make them turn tail and bury themselves like bugs in the grass. What is this dean saying and that dean doing? What are they plotting? My demise, Thomas, my demise. There is a truth and that truth is that everyone and everything is plotting your demise. Remember that. Visit the Dean of the The. Read the reports he sends me at the hour before dawn. The valley is immense and we are alone, he writes, and a wind blows down from the mountains. What does it matter that the mouse cries out to the owl. Nothing matters but the owl's response.

Here, she says and hands me a glass of Frascati. I've written a little parable that you must proof before it's printed.

She leads me to the circular lake of her conference table and before me she places:

A RUMBLING

A rumbling was heard in the night that the old man took to be the rumbling of his wife's teeth in the jar beside him. But he was wrong.

The old woman heard the rumbling too and she took it to be the rumbling of the fetus she had wanted the old man to give her the past fifty years but that he had not given her because he said he did not want anything but himself growing inside his wife. But she too was wrong.

A hole at the back of their heads was causing the rumbling, or rather the trucks that roared out of the dark road of their heads were.

And now other things are coming out of the holes in the heads of the old man and the old woman.

And no one can stop what is coming.

Yes, I think, this should quell the rumors when it's placed in the faculty mailslots. But the President says, No, no. Nothing can do that. But it will quieten the rabble for a spell, and what more of a prose work can one expect? If this parable manages to do that, it will have done enough. I do not wage my battles by pen. I have other means, Thomas, of which you alone are aware.

I nod my assent.

I imagine the President pouring me another glass. The Frascati is cool and pleasantly sharp on my palate, and I suspect on the President's as well.

How many times have I been in this sacred space? Not many. I can still count them on my two hands. But no matter how often I am here, I know that it will never become familiar, never will I take for granted that I have entered the sacred space of the President's chamber. Never will I fail to feel a little chill of power pass from the air into my veins. Never will the clouds outside the window fail to enthrall me with their mobility and mass.

I open the door to her private chambers.

How long have I been standing here speechless?

The President is behind her desk. She does not stand. She offers me a chair which I take.

Outside, dusk settles at the edges of the valley.

You have come to tell me about the rumors, she asks.

8. A Questionnaire

When I return to my cubicle, I find, slipped under my door, the following list of questions in a nondescript hand:

1. If there is no bridge or walkway linking the two Towers, how is it that the President can move so quickly between the two?
2. When was the Dean of the University Archives last seen?
3. How much does the President earn a year?
4. How many trips has the President made during her administration?
5. Is the President's apartment subsidized by the city? the State? the University?
6. What is the percentage of your salary in comparison to the President's?
7. What percentage of the annual budget goes into financing and maintaining the Gestation Chamber?

8. What are you doing in our country?
9. Do you know if the President will run for re-election when her term ends?
10. Do you know what happened to your predecessor?

Before I can even begin to file a report on this missive (surely from the enemies of the President), the Dean of the University Archives enters and snatches the questionnaire from my desk.

An old form, he says, an old script. No one has had to answer these questions in years.

Then why was it put under my door?

The Dean of Archives is old; his teeth, what few are left, are yellowed and wobble when he speaks; his breath smells like cold ashes.

Oh, he says, all foreigners must see it. The form remains, even if the content has been long forgotten.

He rattles the sheet of paper in front of my face, then tucks it into his gray jacket's inner pocket.

Filed under miscellaneous, he says, then vanishes as quickly as he had arrived, leaving behind only the wind from his fluttering coattails.

These strange deans, where did they come from? How long has it taken them to rise from the ranks of professors? Or were they born, so to speak, into their position? If I were the President, I would fire them all, start afresh. But perhaps these old deans support her. This is a possibility. I do not claim to understand, or ever hope to understand, University politics. Bureaucratic weasels, my grandmother used to say. Nothing but snivelling little bureaucratic weasels. After her successful novel, she taught a term at

Radcliffe and could go on for hours about university administrators.

But for me in this strange land, I often can't tell the administrators from the professors. I can find no telltale traits between the one and the other, though perhaps the distinction, which I've yet to learn, is to be found in the cut or color of their robes. Regardless, each group for now is equally strange, equally incomprehensible to me.

They gather in the hallways, these deans and professors, in clusters, like a grove of fir trees in a Swiss forest. They bend toward one another, then spread apart and come together again. In their branches small animals scurry for their nests. I cannot make out what the deans say to one another, their voices are a low, guttural cawing. When I pass, they cluster even tighter together, their voices become silent, their eyes turn so inward I cannot see into them—opaque surfaces that reflect nothing, *sans* intelligence, *sans* meaning. But when I walk by them, their heads move in unison and they stare after me until I leave the hallway.

Perhaps they are considering me as a possible ally, but if they are against the President, if they think I could ever betray my benefactress, they are mistaken. But then why the questionnaire? I do not believe the archivist's version of the event; I do not think such a form is given to every foreign employee of the University. For one thing, I know for a fact that the Gestation Chamber has only been in existence for less than a year. So why lie to me if he didn't think me suspect or that I might suspect him? What byzantine forces are at work here? Does the President know this?

Yes, I am sure she does, and that as I write, she is at work resolving them.

Alone in my white-walled cubicle I have reports to file, I must file reports, that is what I am here for, the President said, and reports I must file. I will find out what I can about this curious University, about the deans and the professors, about her friends and enemies, and, when possible, I will include what I have learned, overheard, uncovered, in my reports. The professors should not underestimate me or the President. But who could possibly underestimate her? Don't they know how, for example, the Gypsy Problem was taken care of? No, this only I know, and who would believe me, and do I even believe it myself? The President leans against the window in the other Tower. She places her forehead against the cold glass. So much to think about, so much to resolve. No one individual, no single human being... Her thoughts go back to her childhood, back to before her childhood, before her birth... So much to do, she thinks, and per-haps only one term left to accomplish it in.

I can no longer see her, the snow is too thick. If only this long winter would end. Then, perhaps, the situation would clear up, her rivals and enemies would flee from the onslaught of the warmth and the sun. But it lingers, it holds like wax to a table, like the snow to the roofs outside my attic window.

I, too, lean against the window; I, too, place my forehead against the cold glass, but still I cannot see her. Only a yellow smudge of light is visible through the office window of the President, a yellow smudge, and something black, a black blur, a blackness stuck in the wintry air, and this blackness breaks loose, flaps its wings, disappears over the S Tower, over the gray shapes of the mountains.

I turn back to my room, to my cluttered desk.

The President stands in the doorway, snow still clinging to her long coat.

You're working overtime again, Thomas, she says.

Yes, ma'am, I say.

Best that you go then, she says, before the snow hides your way home.

9. Language Difficulties

If only I understood the laws of the University, then I might understand why the President could not simply fire all her enemies, but obviously even the President cannot do that. Civil positions, I suppose, with a union as well; whereas my salary comes from the President's Special Fund, with the State supplementing it with health insurance and other benefits, most of which are also beyond my ken. What am I to make of the Undertaking Provision or the Twin Towers Compensation or the White Cloud Tax? These and other notations on my pay stubs mean nothing to me. And the notations change from month to month: the Betrayers' Sentiment becomes the Worker's Loss, the Place Tax becomes the Grounds' Fare. Perhaps my translations are awry, the language of the bureaucracy impenetrable to a non-native speaker, the syntax a fortress within a labyrinth. By the time I've broken the syntactical code, the meaning of the words have flown through the window of its semes. The sentences of Geman bureaucracy are a ghetto of broken rooftops, a mouth with decaying teeth, a dry river bed where scorpions scurry between the cracks in the earth that flakes away like burnt paper. But oddly, when the professors or the deans speak, no matter how thick their Swabian accents, I can follow them with ease, even though their language often is as complicated as the most abstruse official report. Or perhaps it's only their lips that I follow, their German lips that tell me more than their words ever could, that let me into the meaning if not the message behind what they are saying.

Is it essential that I report everything I hear verbatim? The President does not want my reports to be official; she wants them to be free from fear, free from the impress of the Towers' sway. I want your reports fluid, she said. I want your reports to state in as clear a language as you can manage the nature of what it is that interests you in the University. Be free with your language, Thomas, she said. Let the words lead you where they want to go, not vice-versa. You are not in control. Certainly you cannot expect to be in control. You are my assistant. No one can tell you what to do but I. The words will take you down the corridors of the University into the rooms where research occurs, secret research, private discoveries that we have not yet deemed necessary to reveal to the public, our conclusions are incomplete, there are problems we have not yet foreseen, we have our doubts. In these rooms experiments are in progress. Report them to me. Report what you see, what you sense. I am as aware as any of my predecessors that things are going on in the University that are kept from the President. I am not ashamed to admit this. This is part of my job. I must let what occurs occur free of any interference from me, though I have the right to interfere, yes, I certainly have the right. But I will not interfere. Research must go on in an atmosphere free of fear, as must your reports. Only in this way can we ensure growth and development. The concept of a liberal University is dear to me, Thomas, as it should be dear to anyone who works in the University. But this concept is not dear to everyone, no, it is not. My enemies, yes, my enemies do not hold the same beliefs as you and I. Of this I am aware as well. I need your reports to keep me alert. Here, Thomas, in my offices, I am not always in touch with what goes on around me. You need not shake your head, Thomas, my dear boy, my assistant. Even I can lose touch with the University, here in my offices, even I can lose touch with the directions of the winds, the replenishment of which is the top priority of the Deans of Surmise and the Ode. They are in place, are they not, the new Deans of Surmise and the Ode? Good, good. I need you to keep me alert to those aspects of the University that otherwise I would never notice. Soon your reports will be reports from the front. You do not know what I mean, I understand that, but it doesn't matter at the moment. Have you been here long? It seems like only yesterday that I hired you. My previous assistant is no longer with us. I must tell you about him sometime. I had to let him go. Will the same happen to you? I don't think so. You are a good assistant. My speeches you have written have all been a great success, especially the sentence in your Thanksgiving speech that said "If I were an American, I would want to remember on this holiday, no matter how reluctantly, the horrors upon which America was founded, that genocide was not the exception but the policy." Yes, a fine sentence, one that received applause, and I regret you were not there to hear and see the effect of your words. More sentences like that in your speeches would be welcome, but not too many, Thomas, not too many. You cannot grow solely by offending. You must listen to the words themselves. They will tell you what to say, they will tell what is being said, they will tell the truth only you can report back to me.

When she speaks to me in her office, I accept everything she says, but when I come home to my attic apartment, when I sit at my desk that looks out upon the winter-locked city at night, I feel that the President has only been humoring me, that in no way can I really be of help to her Presidency, that she hired me only out of a kindness that I cannot understand, that I am totally inadequate to whatever task she assigns me, that I should write a letter of resignation stating that I am unworthy, someone else surely could be of more use to her, then clear off my desk, clean out my apartment and catch the next flight to Little Rock. But what right have I to question the President's choices? If she should put her faith in my abilities, I can do nothing more than try to meet her expectations. Despite this long winter, despite the rumors at the University, despite the strange deans and the mysteries surrounding the Head-in-Progress and the Gestation Chamber, despite the difficulties of the language.

So I leave my chair beside the window and busy myself in my small kitchen, make another cup of

Abendtraum tea over my small stove. The wind rattles to get into the kitchen, but the window is closed tight. Beneath me the other tenants have already gone to bed. It is late. I can hear the mice who live above me under the roof busy with their nightly foraging. I would leave them some food if I had any to spare. The times are hard and going to be harder. The President has insinuated as much. I must be ready for whatever is to come.

And something is coming, I know it, though I cannot say what it is because I have yet to learn the University's inner workings. Where will my knowledge lead me in the end? Will I wish that I had remained in ignorance back in Arkansas? Such cowardly thoughts I must never express to the President, she certainly would not approve of them. She would want me to face what is to come forthrightly and report promptly (and circumspectly) back to her. But what is to happen to Ihre Magnifizenz and her Presidency? And what to me?

As I lie under the cover of three counterpanes and stare at the mountain in the Friedrich print on the ceiling above me, possibilities terrify me. The mountain is grayish-blue, a pale yellow light hovers above it, but the foot of the mountain is dark with trees. Will I awake someday into this landscape? Will the President take me there? Will she escape the conspiracies weaving around her? Will I?

A night bird calls out, but no one answers. Beside me I have a stack of books, old paperbacks picked up from Tom's Bookstore on Rembrandtstrasse—*City of the Chasch*, *The Metal Monster*, *The Beautiful and*

Dead. Sometimes I read them when I cannot sleep, or I turn on the radio and through the static pick up Radio Romania or Radio Moscow or Radio Ukraine, and listen through the night to languages I cannot understand.

10. The Towers

A low cloud conceals the top floors of the Towers when I arrive early for work this morning. From my cubicle I can see nothing but particles of fog. I want to file a report on the fog, a report on the Towers in the fog, a report on the enemies of the President, a report on the rumors of her impeachment, her dismissal, rumors of her relations with the Mysterium. But the fog lays its gray glove over my thoughts and I can think of nothing except the Towers.

These buildings are their own *raison d'être*, the President once told me, and I was left to make of this statement what I could. Was this on my first day at work? The second?

I was told to explore the buildings by myself for an hour, so I began in the basement. Black leaves swept against my feet as I wandered this dark chamber where thick pillars blocked my view into its depths. Stacks of insulation breathed in the corners. Somewhere I thought I heard the bleating of a goat, and I left the basement in a hurry.

The elevators rumble, as if they were the Tower's

throat, and the building hums with its own meaning while the staff and professors and students hurry
about their business of learning and making and forgoing the inevitable day when they must leave the
University, that dreaded day when they must leave
the Tower and find a purpose that is not pre-ordained.

On any given day the Towers direct us into
our respective spaces—to the S Tower's third floor
where measurement fields are being maintained and
inscribed on the calendar; to the fourth floor where
the ladders that will rest at the base of the Head-in-
Progress are tested for resiliency and rapture; to the
History Department for a class with Herr Professor
Dr. Zurücksinken called "From the Feasts of the
Middle Ages to the Fast-food Culture of Today: A
History of Nutrition"; to Room 11HT where a con-
ference on Emptiness and the Constituents of Its
Avatars has just concluded.

On 4aHT I overheard one Professor Dunkelbach
discussing a bit of Merrittean metaphysics with three
coeds. "Goddess of the Inexplicable! Madonna of the
Metal Babes! The Nursery of the Metal People!" he
read to them, and the students scribbled away in their
official notebooks. The madness of memorization, as
you see, can never harm them, Dunkelbach said. They
are immune to what afflicts us: loss of memory, of
mystery, of delight in the mundane. Take this away,
and what do you have? A music box the President can
wind and rewind until the end of her days.

I wrote all this down, even though I did not
know what it meant. A message in code? A message at
all? And what did Dunkelbach's text under discussion

have to do with the President? Strange words, I thought, but the President I am sure can decipher them. I pocketed my notebook and, without looking further into this curious niche of HT, continued my tour of the Tower.

I had read about the Towers in the University's pamphlets, had read: "Despite their geometric conformity and the grayness of their walls, the air in the Towers often is a greenish haze. When you raise your hand, the air clings to the hand's outline for a moment, before dissolving into itself again. Students and staff entering like windswept leaves, the morning swirling in behind them, voices of construction workers above the clangor of the city, tram sounds, buses, the underground trains, an artist asleep on a park bench, the bench in search of the sun, of warmth, the Tower fills itself with books and protons, draws into its arms the city's dissonance, awakes attentive and without alarm."

But the pamphlets did not help me as I wandered through and between the Towers, hoping to understand the scope of the buildings, the dimensions that I would have to work within, the limits of my responsibilities. These dimensions I would only begin to understand when I better understood the character of the President, understood her own limitations and strengths, though when I think of her limitations I see an open plain stretching out to the horizon beneath which zebras and topi and kudus graze without fear of predators.

I know this is fancy, but it is fancy the President instills in me. She has her enemies. Predators loom just beyond the horizon. The herd is restless, they cock their heads, sniff the wind.

Only the custodians roam the Towers at this time of day. Her enemies are asleep; they are the ones who drag into work, refuse to meet their students. I am only assuming this to be the case, I have no hard evidence it is the case. The world wants us to acknowledge it even when we are asleep. The President's standards are of the highest of any employer I have ever worked for. At my university in Arkansas we had no such President. The president of my university was never seen by us students, whereas the President is on the cover of each issue of the University's newspaper, *Der Turm*, and the students have read her books, have heard her speeches.

When I am alone in my white cubicle and sense the President is not in the Tower (though she may, for all I know, be in the other Tower this morning, may, for all I know, have never gone home, worked all night in her office planning strategies to make the University a better institution of learning for the students and the State), I sense the power of the Towers as they face one another, mirror one another, so that sometimes I mistake S Tower for H Tower and take the elevator to the ninth floor of the Sciences Tower only to discover that where my cubicle should be, there is no door, no window, only a hallway that stretches farther than my eye can see. And when, as now, the tops of the Towers are covered with low clouds, I can imagine that they rise far beyond the eleventh floor, to the twentieth, the hundredth, higher.

Plans perhaps are in the works for the extension upward of the University. The President might like this idea, but, no, there are no new ideas I can give the President. I am not here to present new ideas. There are no ideas the President has not already thought of herself. Of this I am sure. The Towers are themselves filled with ideas that I shall never understand. I imagine them staring at one another at night and during the day the Towers are asleep; they dream while we work, they work while we dream.

I wander the veins of the sleeping HT. A custodian sweeps the fifth floor. Birds flutter against the window, but the Tower does not let them in. Has the fog confused them? I pass the office of the Dean of the University Archives. His door is locked. I pass the office of the Dean of the The. His office has no door, only a curtain. I want to part the curtain. I want to talk to the Dean of the The. It was he alone who smiled at me when the President introduced me, her new assistant, to her deans. Not the Dean of Misalliance, or the Dean of the Seamless, or the Dean of Surveillance, or the Dean of Surgery, or the Dean of Misoneism (whose fearful visage and bloody beak I will never forget), or the Dean of Misprints, or the Dean of Heavenward, or the Dean of Constriction and Construction. The curtain is velvety. Behind it I hear nothing. Is there an office there? An auditorium? A screen?

It is the fog that has led me here. I had other matters to attend to this morning. I had come to work to file my daily report that the President will read, I am sure she reads my reports, each day I file a report or write a speech and I am sure that the President reads every report I give her. Why else has she hired me if not for me to file reports that will at least amuse if not inform her?

The curtain hangs heavy before my eyes, heavy as the eyelids of students at a lecture on capital delivered by octogenarian economists. A hand reaches to part it. The Dean ushers me in.

11. Encounter with a Dean

Ah, yes, says the Dean of the The, it's the President's assistant. Come in, my dear Herr Abjectus, come in, come in. We've been waiting for you longer than you know. Time's not what it used to be, as my colleague Herr Horn tells me everyday as we dine on the Mensa's so-called food. What is, I ask Herr Horn, what is, to which he has nothing to say. We are alone, my boy. We are all alone. Here, yes, take my hand.

He stretches out his hand, a large, curiously flat hand. Like a playing card, an old, wrinkled, grease-spotted playing card, the kind my grandmother used to deal out to me with a flourish of her painfully thin wrist, then lean into my face, her breath a bit rancid from all the garlic in the pasta that night, and say, Herein lies the clue to the game. If you listen to your own thoughts long enough, you can't lose. Then she would cackle and I didn't know whether to believe her or not. The old card shark, I thought, when I looked at my hand, never a card of the same suit, same number, face, gender, never a straight. Night after night of this, for as long as I remember, until she published her novel and the President pulled me out of Chet Darling's Downtown Mobil, lifted me, so to speak, off the Coca-cola rack right into the heart of this pumping thing called the University.

Up and down goes his cold, thin hand in mine, as he leads me into the cavern of his office, a crepuscular tunnel of an office, I can make out little here.

Up and down, but in the mechanical movement of his arm, in the bell-tones of his voice, in the grid-glitter of his eyes, I suddenly remember my first encounter with the Dean of the The. This is not, I think, the man I saw during my orientation, the man who greeted me with the pleasant grip of an insurance executive on the day of his retirement. This is not the man who made me welcome in this foreign university, who knew my language as well, no, better than I, who wrapped his arm around my shoulder and said, "Welcome to the University, as rich a garbage dump as you'll find in this Universe," and winked broadly at me. His body was big, his face meaty and pale, whereas the man in front of me is wafer-thin and tanned.

Come in, he says again, at last releasing my hand, and the tunnel suddenly opens out into an office proper, except I cannot see the ceiling, the darkness swallows it up. I see a desk on which sits a stack of reports whose titles I cannot make out. A cup of coffee steams pleasantly under a green, cone-shaped lamp. In a corner a ficus nods its leaves. On each wall, a door marked ☞EXIT.

Are you…, I begin, but he completes my thought: The Dean of the The? No, no, or rather I am now, or what's left of the position. We've had to consolidate

The and Exclusivity, or rather, better say the latter has assimilated the former. You must be thinking, Herr Schafskopf—you do not mind, do you, if I call you that, a term of endearment that all of us in Exclusivity refer to you with, no offense meant, none allowed, as we so often say…

But why…

Consolidation, Herr Abjectus. Funny name, yours, amusing name, we often laugh together over coffee. How could we not? You do not know the ways of the University. You cannot understand our meetings in public or secret. What are you but another shadow of Ihre Magnifizenz, *die Rektorin*, Frau President. A head without body. A voice, a whisper, a whimper. But cheer up. We are here to assist you, Herr Gehülfe. Even I, here in Exclusivity, want you to know that I am here to help you however I can. This is, after all, what we are placed in this University to do. By-law by by-law by by-law. Let's have more of them, as I always say. What can I do for you?

Rumors, I say, I am today to file a report on the Persistibility and Functionality of Rumors and Their Concurrent Threads in and through the Ways and Byways of the University.

Ah yes, he says and looks around him as if he could pluck the fictitious file from the air or the ficus or the cone-shaped lamp. Here, Herr Abjectus, read this, he said, handing me a file from his desk.

What is it? I ask, staring at the pink transparent folder whose title I cannot make out.

Haven't sent it to the Dean of Authenticity, he says. Not yet, *noch nicht*. But we will soon. Have to.

Nothing to do about it. A rumor or a reality? Can you tell me? Have a look. It concerns your predecessor. A report, perhaps, he filed that has made its way here. We've others. How many? A few. Maybe two. Maybe three. Have a look. It reads well, at least we can say that about it. It doesn't read like your typical report. Which makes us suspicious. But perhaps you can best judge. Really, Herr Bendemann, Herr Kleinchen, Herr Tumbleton, Herr Vanellus vanellus, really, my good sir, what do you expect it is that goes on in these niches and corridors of the University that only she, Ihre Magnifizenz, should have access to? But that is not my department, only a clearing house, only a clearing house, as my children shout at me each morning as I rush off to catch the S-bahn to work. Have a look. It won't hurt you. Perhaps you would like to authenticate it? Well, no matter. We have experts. We have reports to file, too. Don't forget that. We are not lame, not consumptive, ha, no, after all, we are what we are, good and steady civil servants who once professed to profess more than we knew, until we learned a better way. Have a look. Why not? What can it hurt? And then, Herr Thomas, I will take you to the Room of the Activated Eye, our latest project, not yet off the ground, only a beginning, but one that you especially will want to be familiar with. Oh, not that the President doesn't know all about it. Of course she does, our President, for whom, I want you to know, I voice loudly and clearly my support.

I tell him I am glad to hear it and that I will inform Ihre Magnifizenz at the next opportunity of his support.

Fine, fine, he says. Perhaps she will welcome a new perspective, one not entirely tainted by her—and here, Herr Abjectus, I must drop to a whisper—enemies. Yes, even I know that she has her enemies, that plans are fermenting, have been ever since she was elected, and especially since she was re-elected. But now there are other matters to concern ourselves with, not that they do not have a bearing, for indeed they do, Herr Abjectus, indeed they do, on what we have just discussed. I hope you are not offended that I have been so forward with you. We have, let me say it now, confidence in your ability to report back to the President everything you see and hear and read. We expect it; we wish it. So, Herr Menschenaffe, have a look at the report. Take your time. Not too much time, thank you. Not what it used to be, as the old song goes. Have a look. Take your time, not mine. Ha. Herr Abjectus. Ha! I'll be back, he says. Have a look, if you can, have a look and let us know what you think, let the President know what you think, that is all we ask, for now.

As I listen to these last words, the room seems to grow darker, the walls dim, the air coalesces to a point a few feet from my face, and I can no longer see the Dean of Exclusivity, as if he has been swallowed up by the room.

The folder hums in my hand.

Alone now, I open it.

12. "Report to the Committee of Alterity"

Someone above (below? next to?) me is playing the piano. Is it the President? Does she know the "Gnossiennes"? I do not think so, but how can I be sure? Shall I ask her when we next have dinner?

Yes, I have been dining more often with the President. When we meet for dinner, she always wears red and knows exactly where she wants to eat. She orders for me, and since I am not Swabian, I am grateful that she does. Tonight at the Zeppelin-Stüble she orders asparagus with Hollandaise and a liter or a liter and a half of white wine. She is interested in my proposal for changing the route I take to work each morning. Yes, she says, the U-Bahn on alternate Mondays. One can never be too careful. A good idea.

I admire the President. Yesterday, she tells me, she fired the Dean of Protocol and Impossibility. My knife is having a hard time cutting the asparagus, but I am not, as I said, of this region and not averse to making a mess of things. He told me, she says, I would live to regret my action. I told him that I already did, but the fact remained that he was simply not the person for the job. He was very angry, almost in tears, she says. The President watches me struggling with the asparagus and drinks more wine.

I, as I said, admire the President. I've never seen anyone enjoy power as much as she. She tells me that she has a plan to make over the faculty senate. And what is this plan, I ask. I, she says, will spring it on them when the time comes.

The President is of average height, not too short, not too tall, more tall than short, but not too tall, but when I return to my one-room apartment directly below her five-room apartment, she appears in my mind's eye even taller. Her hair is pulled back so tight on her head it is hard to judge its length, and her dresses all flare, and this makes her seem even larger.

The President is screaming. We are missing page 171, we are missing page 171! The office stirs, the Towers tremble, sag, merge in memory. Everyone scatters in search of the missing page. The missing page is not in the alcove. It is not in the wastebaskets. It is not in the Zone of Zones. An attributable cyclone, says one dean. A thief, says another. My father is no longer with us, says another. We are alone, we all say. But the President is not appeased. Page 171 is missing, page 171 is missing! she screams and slams her tight fist onto her desk. The secretaries huddle in the corner. The President glares. The President fumes. I await the ritual sacrifice.

And now she is talking of firing her chancellor. A disgusting man, she says. He simply can't do his job. And what plan, I ask, has she to accomplish this task? I, she says, will go to the minister and say, Minister, it's either him or me. Will that work, I ask. The President looks at me as if to say, You must be kidding, then laughs and says, Yes, of course it will.

It's gray and cold this morning. Light rain mixed with snow drifts down off the mountain into the city. Above me the President is preparing for her day, but I do not have to prepare. I only have to await her instructions. As always, her agenda is full, I am sure. A meeting here and a meeting there and more meetings to come. Stay close, she says. I am grateful for anything she says.

In our apartment building I never see the President. She lives in the apartment directly above mine and she passes the door of my apartment at least twice a day, but I never meet her in the hall or on the elevator. Is she hiding from me? Am I hiding from her? Each morning and each evening I hear the sound of high-heeled shoes tapping down and up the stairs, and though I believe this is she going and coming, I can not say for sure.

The President's office is huge and filled with light. A long conference table is in one corner overlooked by an abstract painting, slashes of black on white. Her desk has a transparent glass top, and on it is a minimalist halogen lamp and a notepad and a silver pen in a drinking glass. In the corner rustles a large ficus plant.

Quietly the President prepares herself for her agenda-packed day. I hear her door open, close, the sound of her heels on the stairs. At the sink, I turn off the water so as not to disturb her departure.

Does the President, I wonder, like me? I have, to my knowledge, done nothing to anger her, but sometimes, still, I wonder if she does not find me, in ways I cannot fathom, wanting. I do my job as best as I can, and when I offer suggestions, as I have recently done, I do so as inconspicuously as possible. And never has she allowed me to pay for one of our meals.

She likes to tell the story of how, when she was applying for her first job, a former professor of hers said that she would be hired over his dead body. She pauses, holds up her wine glass as if to display the dance of the candle's reflection, and says, Then I was hired and the old goat croaked.

I notice that when we meet over dinner that she repeats herself. Several times she has told me about the professor who died when she was hired. I laugh at what she says, wondering if my laughter is the same as it was the time before, and then I tell her about the first time I was fired, and when she begins to laugh, I realize that I, too, have told this story to her two or even three times before.

Tonight it is raining when we leave the restaurant. The President takes my arm as we walk up the hill. We are both a bit drunk, and I have the sense, as she clings to me, that she is holding me up as much as I am her. At my door she tells me that we must do this again, and I agree. Then she walks up to her apartment and I fumble my key into the hole and enter my one-room apartment and then lie in bed hearing nothing above me and wonder if she will ever take me out to dinner again.

The Dean of Exclusivity stares at me from across his desk.

What does he expect from me? Does he imagine I will somehow be swayed by this foolish report? Does he think I was in any way swayed by his own meretricious mumbling about the President?

I place the file firmly on his desk.

This is not, I say with conviction, the President I know.

13. In the Outer Office

The President is nowhere to be found! And I with all these rumors in my head, raging there, multiplying, following one another down a corridor at whose end stands a waist-high ashtray shaped like an upside-down question mark.

Where is she? Her secretary stares blankly at me. She does not know, she says. Then she smiles a closed-mouth smile I cannot fathom.

But I must tell the President something. I must. I am her personal assistant.

We know who you are, says the secretary, but I simply cannot oblige you, dear Herr Personal Assistant. She did not come in today, we have no word.

How can that be? This has never happened before, I say.

Ah, the secretary says pointing a pencil at me, its sharpened tip catching for a moment the fluorescent light, but you have only been here a short time, Herr Thomas, only a short time, and you know little of the President's comings and goings. Just wait, the

President will turn up when you least expect her, and then you must be ready, as I am ready at all times. "At station" I like to think of it. At station. I am always at station, for I too do not know where the President might, so to speak, fetch up, what demands she might at any moment make on me, what new article to type, what command to issue, what objectives to send to the copier for immediate dissemination, what translation to turn into German, Romanian, French, what train to track down, what reservation at what restaurant to make, bills to pay for purposes stated or unstated, public or private, it matters not. I, simply, must be at, so to speak, my station, ready and, let us say, willing, for above all being "at station" means being willing to do whatever is asked of me, as, surely, you, too, must know, Dear Herr Gehülfe. "At station" is my motto, my credo, my quiddity, whether you recognize it as such or not. *Verstehen Sie?*

I nod, for I indeed do know, or think I know, or have dreamed similar sentiments as the ones expressed by the President's secretary.

But what I have to see the President about is more important than anything I have yet encountered in my work at the University. I must tell the President what Exclusivity showed me, where I was taken, what strange developments are in progress here, ones that perhaps she herself is not aware of, her enemies must have planned them, she must know immediately what it is I have been told and seen.

My dear Herr Fremdeskind, the secretary continues, drawing spirals in the air with the pencil still pointed at me, you must not think you are so special.

71

TOM WHALEN

What makes you think you are special? You are not, cannot, never will be special here at the University. You are, yes, the President's assistant, but don't you know you are one of among many assistants. We are all, at this university, the President's, in a manner of speaking, assistants, ready to do as she wishes, ready to sacrifice our time, duties, career, perhaps even lives, yes, perhaps, who knows, our lives, for the President. So do not think in any way, even if you are her *personal* assistant, you are unique.

I had no desire to argue with the President's secretary, no desire really even to be standing in front of her desk behind which hovered a huge ficus in whose limbs I thought I saw the speckled body of a thrush (alive? stuffed? the bird did not move). I wanted only to find the President. I had things to tell her about the Dean of Exclusivity, about the Activated Eye, about the Head-in-Progress. And I had as well a few questions to ask her. Was it possible that she was unaware of all this? Did she know of the existence of the Alterity report? Was this report fact? fiction? Her enemies were working late into the night on projects that I could only faintly comprehend, vaguely imagine. What knowledge did she have of them?

Dear Frau Secretary—and she nods her golden hive of hair toward me, taps her red lips with the pencil tip—might you oblige me at least so far as to let me peruse, if it's not any trouble or in any way inappropriate or unseemly, the President's daily itinerary?

Certainly, she says, and hands it over.

Quickly I run my eyes over her plans for the day:

8.00 Breakfast with the Deans of Immateriality and Immortality—discuss their intention before lunch of honoring the Agenda in the presence of all the participants of the QWFQ Minutes to the Steering Committee, Hong Kong Meeting.

8.30 Astronomical matters.

9.00 "Pipelining."

9.30 "Incubation" versus "Centering."

10.00 Resolution of the "open" way proposed by "Balloon" and its constituents before haunting of halls and dissent begins. Consult Deans of Neuroscience and Happenstance before ordination of Biomechanics.

10.30 H-P.

11.00 H-P continued but not concluded.

12.00 Lunch with subdeans and potential backups for Design and Transference who as of yet do not know they are backups "in-clover" as well, heh, heh. Add logistical support. Liaison office awaits further calls, but delay until the end or an even later date.

12.15 Award ceremony for retiring professors about to become Prof. Emeriti in Clear Structures. Speech #123539 34853-29523.

13.00 Meeting with Per. ass. Vital information for continuance. Report. Assessment. Directions and beyond.

13.00 hours! That was now. Now was 13.00! She was supposed to meet me now!

The room swirled, the agenda fluttered out of my hands back onto the green lake of the Secretary's desk. For a moment the duration of which I cannot specify, a meaningless mantra went through my head—One met one and I am alone,

one met one and I am alone, one met one and I am alone, et cetera.

You see, the Secretary smiled up at me, interrupting my empty chant, you were on time. I congratulate you, but alas the President has yet to come in. You were the first, you see, to come into the office today. No one else has entered the door. The office is lonely, no calls, no messages, no President, no visitors, not even the Dean of Disturbance who inevitably interrupts my lunch, not even him, though for years, decades, we have made love, I and the Dean of Disturbance, here on my desk, there on the chair, and always the bird observes unmoving and unmoved—a remarkable phenomenon. But no phenomenon is as rare, unique, if you will, than that of the President's not showing today, of all days, her favorite of the week, the month, the year. Surely you know why, dear Herr Per. ass., surely you of all people know the importance of today to Ihre Magnifizenz. Yes, yes, you of all the ones who have had the good fortune to work for the President knows that today is February 22nd, that most blessed of days, birthday of the idea from which sprung this institute's conception from the mind of a dark traveller when he glimpsed moonlight in a mountain pool beneath him as he crossed the Hugo Mountain. Surely you know how the President honors this day of all days. And, yes, it is true that at this hour, 13.00, she had scheduled a meeting with you, a meeting whose significance I know nothing of except its utmost importance. And yet, still, you see, Herr

Pferdli, she is not here, has not been in all day, and she does not answer the phone in her apartment, nor does she answer the phone in the office of the other Tower. I have tried on the hour, yes, I have tried, but to no avail, no avail.

Her words rustle the leaves of the ficus—or is it the wind coming from beneath the door of the President's office? I see a light there, a cold light, but behind it no one stirs.

A quiet day, as I said, for me, she says, a lonely one. I thank you for your visit, but I cannot ask anything more of you. Forgive me for asking so much. The agenda confused me as it confused you, I must admit, but I am only the President's secretary and you are only her personal assistant, and what is that? Nothing, or almost nothing, compared to the life of the President and the demands on her.

I bow before you—and she bends her head so far that her forehead touches the desktop, her golden hive a swirl of glitter and darkness down which for a moment I feel I might fall like Alice, but no cat or denial will let me fall upward out of dream, and the rest of what she says is lost to me.

Then there is silence in the room.

She does not move.

An hour has passed.

The President, I decide, is not coming.

And she has met none of her appointments for the day? I ask her secretary.

None, she pertly replies.

And no one has complained?

You're the first, she says.

Well then, I say, thank you.

Don't mention it, she says. I'll tell her you called. And Herr Abjectus?

Yes?

Please close the door on your way out.

14. The Activated Eye

For hours, it seemed, after I left the President's secretary, I wandered the corridors in search of the President. I rode the elevators, climbed the stairs, pried open broom closets, slipped into rooms of darkness and lectures, examination rooms where students were lined against the wall and made to recite the standard history of the University over and over. There was the Room of Scribbling outside of which I could hear the scrabbling of pencils over paper, like the mice feet my grandmother and I would listen to every night back in Cooter Neck during those first few weeks after the death of my parents and long before she published her novel, but when I opened the door, I could see no one in the room, no student at the bolted-down tables, could only hear the sound of writing. The Room of Music, on the other hand, bulged with the bodies of professors and students, none of whom would even glance at me when I asked them if they knew the whereabouts of the President, so intent were they on the performance (how long had it been going on?) of Satie's "Vexations."

Other rooms about which now I can only recall random images: *Der Zettelraum*, or Room of Snippets; the Monument Room, its lavender wallpaper imprinted with egrets and obelisks; the Room of the Fainting Women; the Room of Toes; the Room of Nothingness with its nailhead floor.

Finally, defeated and exhausted, I gave up and returned to 9aHT.

Alone in my tiny cubicle, my President's location unknown, all I can do is report on what has occurred. This is what she would want; this is, after all, my primary job. I must report to the President even when I do not know where she is or whether she will ever read what I write. This is all I can do now that I am alone again in my soft, white, tiny cell. All I can do is write my report, reports, and hope that somehow they will find their way into the President's hands before it is too late. How melodramatic that must sound, but unfortunately how apposite.

This is what I recall: The Dean of Exclusivity introduced me to the Dean of Dramaturgy who led me to the office of the Dean of Conflation who took my hand and opened a door, and I saw what I thought at first was a painting of a huge eyelid, and then I thought I saw the eyelid tremble, jiggle, then slap up like a windowshade and open out like a rose.

Then the rose closed into an iris, and within the iris I saw clouds luffing in a blue sky and their shadows spreading over a snow-covered field.

The Activated Eye, our newest addition in our war on ignorance, Herr Assistant, I heard the Dean of Conflation say.

And then my feet sank into the snow and I heard a voice (my own?) chanting, White, white, all is white.

The tracks of hares spiralled out from me, disappearing in the distant fir forest whose trees were coated with snow. Ice sparkled and shimmered, though there was no wind, only a cold so cold my bones felt crystalline. The air smelled of pine and ice and burning wood.

In this endless realm, surrounded by hills of snow-laden firs, my feet crunched the hard snow I know not how long. The sun never set, the snow never fell, only clouds of ice appeared and then vanished against the whiteness, white on white, like a fata morgana.

Once I saw a blackbird flap up from a fir tree and scrive a hieroglyph against the sky. Once I thought I saw the shadow of a huge bird, but when I looked up, it was only a cloud in the shape of a bird.

I walked on and on, my feet sinking deep in the snow, saw the ice-shagged limbs as fine as porcelain, as delicate as the china in my grandmother's glass cabinet, but when I would walk with her and her dog Buster, we were accompanied by smoke from chimneys, by the whuffling of horses in their warm barns, but here was nothing except the snow and myself and the firs on the hills and the horizon.

Finally the light began to fade, though the sun, a cold coin, stayed well above the horizon. The air turned colder, a haze hung over the hills, enveloped the trees, until I seemed to be walking inside an eye gone old and covered in cataracts. My feet did not want to lift out of the snow any longer, every step slower, ever breath harder to take, until I could go no farther, could no longer move. My knees sagged, and I dropped into the snow.

I dreamed then I was in the snow dreaming, and in my dream I was dreaming in a room of no time, no life, no distinction, and I could hear voices all around me.

When the emptiness is finally locked in, then we can proceed.

Only then?

Not before.

But soon?

Before gestation, yes. And we will have them all with us. No one will say no.

Except her.

Her alone.

Within the Activated Eye.

What do you think, Herr Thomas?

I blinked awake and blinked again, and was out of the Activated Eye.

But what is it, what does it do? I asked after the snow scene and its dream vanished. What is it for? I asked the Dean of Conflation.

You mean whom, don't you, Herr Schneeglöckchen, he said, and spread his long, spider-monkey arms, at the ends of which dangled tiny fleshy paws heavy with emerald rings.

For everyone, for everyone! he said with a shout.

But seriously, Herr Schneeflocke, we do not yet know the potential of the Eye, do not know exactly what it can or even wants to do. Our achievement has

not yet been fully assessed, but we have a committee working on it, and undoubtedly you will see, in
the near future, as it passes across your desk, assuming you are privy to such matters, a report from the
Assessment Committee that will explain to you the
benefits of the Eye in the war we are constantly wag-
ing (as per Presidential Directive #23-408520-4850-
3498523-40592332) on ignorance, all rumors to the
contrary. Ignore them, if you can, or assign them to
the trashbin of your imagination, assuming you have
one, for this is the first in a new series of innovations
we hope to bring out of Conflation, in conjunction
with Dramaturgy and Metallurgy, Consolidation and
Exclusivity. We are, I cannot be too explicit about
this, the avant garde in the fight to solve the problems
of Excess Activity to No Avail, of Whistling in the
Corridors, of Fallen Signs. The students, we assure
you, will never be the same. The President will, at the
very least, be amused, and surely you know the importance of this to the continuance of the President's
reign, you of all, how shall I say, people. I mean you
are her personal assistant, are you not, so who better
... But et cetera, Herr Herr, et cetera, as my late predecessor used to say. You have gone far, I believe, in
understanding our position, and in the future it may
become necessary for you to recall your visit to the
Eye, to recall our conversation, this moment in my
office, these shelves, those model ships free of dust,
this anchor-shaped lampstand. That is, we may need
testimony from you, Herr Assistant. Yes, that time
may come when you will be called to readdress your
loyalties.

Perched atop his desk, he smiled down upon me, and on his breath I could smell, faintly, a touch of Frascati. Had he been drinking only a few moments before with the President? At the time I didn't think to question him, but now I wish I had. Perhaps his answer would have resolved more than I know. But I said nothing, only nodded in as non-committal a fashion as I could muster.

He returned my nod, then the intercom on his desk buzzed.

Conflation, he said into the speaker.

Exclusivity, it replied. Finished?

Yes.

Then it is resolved?

To our complete satisfaction, he said, smiling and nodding toward me, and smiling even broader when I smiled and nodded back.

And we may proceed?

As you see fit.

Without further ado.

Without haste or waste.

Or posthaste.

Thank you.

The wall.

I watched it dissolve before my eyes.

15. "Final Report"

Read this. It's by your predecessor.

In the room I had walked into, a man with a face like corrugated cardboard handed me a sheaf of paper. I glanced down at the title: "Final Report as Requested by Intransigence Committee 11/11/__." At the bottom of the title page I saw the President's signed initials and the words, "Preliminary Recital for Reshaping of Room AAAA before Commencement." Over this someone had stamped CONFIDENTIAL.

Where did you get this? I asked. Such documents are not for general use.

We're the Committee on Confidentiality, the man said.

What did he mean by "we"? The two of us were the only ones in the room that I had stepped into from the dissolving wall in the Dean of Conflation's office.

By we, he said, I mean Conflation, Dramaturgy, Metallurgy, Consolidation and Exclusivity, and myself, Sedation—among others I could but shall refrain from naming. Please read the report, Herr Tumbleton, said the Dean of Sedation (or had he said Sedition?).

Did I have a choice? Could I turn back now, right when I felt that I was gathering essential information that would help me not only in my report on rumors, but perhaps even help me to save the President's presidency?

I turned over the title page and began to read, and it did not take long for me to see that its curious style differed distinctly from that of the "Report to the Committee of Alterity."

At my final meeting I was accused of arrogance, but I said that what I was exhibiting wasn't arrogance, I said I was from Texas. No one laughed, but the point was made again by Herr Leerkopf [*] that if he had offered such proposals as I had (modest proposals, ones the University I thought would, without doubt or hesitation, welcome) when he was a guest laborer in Tucson, he certainly would have been accused of Teutonic arrogance. Herr Oberschuhe nodded, as did Herr Hirschmann, Herr Kleinseele, and Herr Getanze. The President only smiled at me, which I took as a sign (an indecipherable sign, as it turned out) and which I returned.

Glasses of Frascati were distributed all around with which we refreshed ourselves and allowed the tension in the chamber to wax or wane according to the temperament of the members. I continued.

I said that the "Head" proposal was certainly worth all of our attention, that I was grateful that the President had asked me to speak to such an esteemed body, that I was, yes, only a youth just barely out of my blue jeans and university in east Texas, and I did not want anyone to consider me arrogant if I proceeded. [Nods of general agreement all round that I proceed.] Good, I said. Thank

[*] All names have been changed in "Final Report as Requested by Intransigence Committee 11/11/__" and the position titles eliminated, except for the President's. (Eds.)

you, I said. Then I said, Experimental investigation of pollutant formation in flames (600 kWth oil/gas, 350 kWth coal dust with milling) with which we had been concerning ourselves over the past year, along with the study of NOx control technologies (fuel and air-staging) had indeed led us to obtain the devolatilization reactor with hot gas separation and burnout reactor, but that our in-flame diagnostics, including Laser-Doppler-Anemometry and our investigation of dust-laden two-phase had as a consequence suffered. I further said that if we concentrated on the mathematical modeling of flames and furnaces first proposed by my predecessor, may he in rest in peace, then we might at last arrive at functionable Finite Element and Finite Volume Codes in two-dimensional polar coordinates and three-dimensional cartesian coordinates that would do us and the University proud.

Herr Leerkopf sipped his wine, requested (politely, I must add) if I needed my glass refreshed (I did), then countered that measuring techniques for emissions and immissions from flames, furnace and automotive engines, as well as the study of reduction technologies for pollutant emissions, which had been, he wanted to emphasize, the department's strengths *since time immemorial*, along with tether balloon measurements of pollutants in vertical profiles, should remain our focus for the next decade. As he spoke, Herr Leerkopf rolled his large body back and forth, favoring his left shoulder (a recent accident on the slopes of Davos), and now he tilted his head toward me and bathed me with his flabby, condescending visage.

I wanted to reply once again that my proposals were modest and that no progress would ever be made if Finite Element and Volume Codes especially in three-dimensional cartesian coordinates were not seriously taken into account. But then Herr Oberschuhe, the department's newest member and formerly from the eastern region of Germany, and whom I had always considered somewhat shy, surprised me by saying that the phrase *since time immemorial* had been used on him at every turn and opportunity and he thought that it was indicative of the

University's central problem which my proposal, albeit in a foreign and uncultured manner, was trying to address.

This, too, for a moment brought the meeting to a standstill and we all looked at our wine glasses and pondered perhaps our curious natures and the uniqueness, if I may, of this meeting, a meeting whose likes had never been seen before at the University.

Then Herr Hirschmann said he agreed with his young colleague's statement, but added that he had been requesting since time immemorial (Herren Leerkopf and Getanze lightly laughed) four fully automatic movable measuring stations for multicomponent air quality investigations and would like this discussed before those of the visitor (he was referring to me, although I had been with the President for a year) were considered. Tether balloon measuring systems for hydrocarbons and meteorologic parameters were all to the good, as were Laser-Doppler-Anemometry and Argon-Ion Lasers (no one had mentioned Argon-Ion Lasers, which led me to wonder if Herr Hirschmann had been paying attention at all to the meeting), but that four automatic movable measuring stations were essential if the Head were ever to be conceived, much less implanted and implemented, and he simply did not see (I am using his exact words) how it was possible for him to continue to work under such *appalling* (he stressed appalling) conditions.

Well, no one said anything for a moment, but I watched the President to see how she would handle this delicate moment, and wasn't disappointed when she said that four automatic movable measuring stations were under advisement and being seriously considered and that as we spoke compromises were in the works at the Office of Budget and Management and that in the meantime we were to make do as best we could (her tone of voice implied that our best was better than anyone else's best) with our entrained flow pyrolysis reactors with their small combustion chambers and, of course, our stellar tether balloon measuring systems. Herr Getanze and Herr Hirschmann did not appear impressed, so the President added that we must not forget (now her voice was firm) that we had been allotted five DEC 5000/200 worksta- tions, three of them with graphics processors, four DEC stations 2100, all coupled in an Ethernet-based LAN with direct access to the Central Computing Center (CRAY 3 supercomputer). After she said this, Herr Getanze and Herr Hirschmann sheepily looked at one another and sipped their Frascati.

That's when I felt it the right moment for me to contin- ue with the rest of my proposal, so I leapt in and said that during my stay here I had noticed all kinds of problems ranging from facilities to qualifications to target groups (most important in my opinion) to principal areas of work to interdepartmental communication, and that I would like to add to my initial proposal of further research in Finite Element and Finite Volume Codes in two-dimensional polar coordinates and three-dimensional cartesian coor- dinates an extension of the tether balloon measurements of pollutants in vertical profiles to include more ambient air investigations over highways and in towns and in homes and over drive-ins, especially the latter where I thought a resurgence could be manifested if the right constituency were targeted. Then I said that best of all would be the introduction of the "Head" into our field of study and measurement localities. I thanked them again for letting me speak of the "Head," that I was pleased that they saw enough benefit in the concept to allow me to talk to them. The members of the committee glowered. The President smiled. By "Head," I said, let me make clear that I mean a head of n dimensions (n being any number of any size in any dimension that all but overstepped the mind's ability to comprehend it) and this head should be 1) bald, 2) possessed of a mouth and ears and eyes and eyebrows in proper proportions and part of a neck and that 3) ladders should rest at the base of the skull and the cheeks to allow the measurers the means to gather the information taken in by the ears and eyes and mouth and nose and that 4) messages should be inscribed upon the skull to alert the angels who would surely be interested in our measuring instrument (i.e., Head) in a code to be decided by another committee, since we were, all in all, not the committee best suited for inventing codes, though we could handle the actual inscribing, that 5) perhaps the best committee to handle the formulating of the messages would be the Adhesion Committee, but that would be open to discussion, and that 6) should angels then appear, and I was sure they would, I, being the instigator of the Head Project, would want to be immediately informed, so that I might have a chance to see the fruits of the Head Project and have the opportunity to establish a communication link (here, I said, we could acquisition a Novell-based PC-LAN with several 386/486 PC's thrown in) with the angels.

I was a little out of breath, a little shaky, even though I was sitting down, but felt that I had made my case forcefully and forthrightly and of course in good faith. Everyone was silent, even the President who was staring at her outspread hands.

Then Herr Kleinseele, who hadn't said anything up to now, said, Arrogance, if we may, may we return to the arrogance that my colleague Herr Leerkopf detected or declaimed evident in the beginning (Herr Kleinseele's English wasn't as good as the others'), it is time, is it not, to reconsider the previously tabled arrogance of the visiting laborer.

The rest of the meeting was something of a blur and flurry of accusations and misunderstandings regarding my intentions that, try though I did, I could not clarify.

Finally, my clothes were stripped from me, and I was carried into a room and laid on a glass table. The lights were switched off. The room went totally dark. The voice of the President said, Dear Herr Assistant, I am sorry.

ADDENDUM

Q. Is what you have written in your final report true?
A. To the best of my knowledge.
Q. The President encouraged you to make these

proposals?

A. She told me that I should begin to assert myself more, that I had been in her employ long enough for her to see that I had ideas that should be shared with the rest of the University, especially regarding the Head-in-Progress project.

Q. Were you told that this would be part of your job when you were hired as her personal assistant?

A. No.

Q. Why are you in a wheelchair?

A. Because my kneecaps are shattered.

Q. Why do you wear dark glasses?

A. Because I can no longer see.

Q. Thank you for your time, Herr Speisereste.

A. (. . .)

I handed the report back to the Dean of Sedation.

Quite fanciful, I said. *Speisereste*, that means leftovers, yes?

He rose from his chair, rose higher and higher, until the room began to swirl around me.

Kommen Sie mit, he said.

16. A Winding Corridor

But was this fancy? Was this report simply another means for the President's enemies to discredit her and the Head-in-Progress project which I had heard so much about? Or was this at last the true story of my predecessor's dismissal that the President herself had refrained from revealing to me? And was this the path down which all her assistants must go? Was I, too, eventually to be introduced into the inner workings of the University only to find myself someday in a dark room, strapped down to a glass table?

I followed the Dean of Sedation down a winding corridor thick with fog, my doubts and fears hurrying after me. The hallway twisted to the left, the right, stretched straight ahead into the haze. Sometimes I lost sight of the Dean of Sedation altogether, could only see the trail left in his wake, a pattern of his body, and hear the rumpling of his coat like a sheet in the wind.

The President. Where was she? Had she been abducted? Had she abdicated? Would I find myself without a job in the morning? But these possibilities seemed altogether mundane when I recalled the power of the President. Perhaps she was in hiding, meditating, gathering her inner resources so she could turn the Faculty Senate again to her desires. The President I knew had resolved the Gypsy Problem. My President someday would stage the lift-off of the first Clown Rocket whose cone contains the spectral seeds of other universities. My President's gaze penetrated the world, penetrated deep into the hearts of her enemies who she well knew wished her great harm. No, no, none of it was true. The "Final Report As Requested by Intransigence Committee 11/11/__" was a lie designed to turn me against her.

I had followed the Dean of Sedation because by so doing I might gain further information for my report on the President's enemies. They were, after all, everywhere. In every office, every classroom, every auditorium, WC, closet, her enemies gathered and concocted plans for her dethroning.

Why had she not left some word for me? Always before, whenever she wanted me, I would know it, somehow I received word—a message left in my campus box, slipped under my door, a wave from the other Tower, a middle-of-the-night tremor, a wind, a cloud. Yet now I knew nothing except that a group of deans (how large exactly I could not say) were going to extreme lengths to show me aspects of the University I had not known existed. Perhaps this, too, was all part of the President's plans for me, her personal assistant plucked from the backwoods of ignorance and placed in a position beyond his abilities. Or perhaps, dare I even think it, the President's enemies were not *my* enemies, they wanted to help me, they knew things about the President I did not know, they would expose me to the nightmare that was the President's reign.

Doubts, dreams, swirled about me in this "vast interior dimness" (the words are James's from *The Princess Casamassima*, as the President surely knows). The city at night from my attic window. The city speckled with white lights, blue and red neon signs whose letters changed throughout the night, from LG to LOGO to GL to LO to OG to OO beneath the leaden, cloud-wracked sky. It would snow again soon. Had it ever stopped snowing? It would continue snowing until the streets were deep with it, until the doors could no longer be pushed open, until the valley itself filled, the mountains vanished, the world. An impenetrable fog overwhelmed the earth, yellowish, cold, indeterminate. This was nothingness, the nothingness I had read so much about in my grandmother's famous novel, a nothingness so absent it covered everything, and of this nothingness nothing else could be said.

I gave myself up to these images as if to providence and wondered what greater providence I could not see loomed ahead. The corridor grew narrow, the walls black and of a height I could not discern. Memories of my grandmother in Cooter Neck, of faces covering the walls, each ancestral visage more dreadful than the one before. (Dread in the marrow of their corrupt, rancid bones, my grandmother would say.) Hideous women in gray hoods pacing up and down stony courts, students marching around and around on the concrete between the two Towers, between Humanities Tower and Sciences Tower, between the H Tower and the S Tower. Which one was I in now? H or S? S, I thought, though I did not remember crossing over.

Circular cells, deep shafts that fell into nowhere. Peepholes through which I caught glimpses of lab technicians climbing up and down ladders. The haze had turned gray, the walls were without dimension or color. I didn't know what time it was. Mid-afternoon? Midnight? Then a fatigue overcame me. Fatigue and dumbness to all things. Nothing mattered. Not even the President? No, not even her. I wanted only to stop, to give in, *Gib's auf, Gib's auf*, the gallery at the back of my brain chanted and tossed their paper cups half-filled with Frascati onto the slumped figure at the podium, jeered and tore up their books and flung them in the air where they took flight like pigeons from a palace roof..., until the custodians turned up the lights and the audience quieted down.

Hours spent in that strange, endless corridor following the Dean of Sedation to where I did not know, following his long, dark, cape-like coat, his shadow, specter, trace, as it made its way through the green haze, into regions I did not know existed in the University. As if I were lost in some curious dream that only a child could imagine, a child who should be dreaming of ponies in open fields, but instead somehow was having a dream of his future, a grid slipped over his present from another time, another place, but the child did not understand this, could not see that the dream was a direction and a warning.

Still with us, Herr Abjectus, the Dean said, and I said, Yes, of course, right here, wouldn't miss it for the world, not for the world, whatever it is you are taking me to. You realize, of course, that you have not told me where we are going, nor did you explain— as if no explanation were necessary!—what my so-called predecessor's "Final Report as Requested by Intransigence Committee 11/11/__" was supposed to mean to me. Was it meant as a warning? Well, dear sir, warnings are always welcome, especially to an outsider such as I, to whom the University often appears a bit, how shall I say, odd and not at all like my university back in Arkansas where such corridors did not, I do not believe, though I can't say with absolute confidence (I recall underground passages from building to building, I recall a greenhouse, a planetarium), exist. But surely, Herr Dean, you did not think I could accept unquestioningly "Final Report as Requested by Intransigence Committee 11/11/__." Such strange names! Was I supposed not to doubt them? Ha, I said. Hardly, I said. The President does not concern herself with my ideas, nor do I offer any. I am not here for the manufacture of new ideas. I leave such activities to you Deans, who are degreed or desperate or deluded or diligent or dreamy enough to do it. I'm here simply to serve the President by filing reports on what I see and hear in the University, but in no way are my reports meant to be objective. They cannot be. I am here, I assume, on an interim basis, whereas the President will go on forever, or so I have been led to believe. Nothing in the new by-laws as of 12/13/__ would lead me to think that the President cannot be voted into office an indefinite number of times, and nothing I have seen would indicate she is in any way in trouble of losing her position. Unless you, of course, have information otherwise.

The Dean of Sedation smiled at me.

You're bluffing, he said.

What?

And then he walked faster, I could barely keep up with him, the fog cleared, and the corridor opened out and up, seemed to twist upon itself, to fold in like a flower, then became a platform, then a ramp that rose higher and higher.

When we reached the top, I panting at the Dean of Sedation's side, we looked down a steep concrete incline into a vast interior dimness, into a cavernous and curious room.

17. The Head-in-Progress

From a distance, at least for a moment, it looked like an ordinary head, though of great dimension. Swept down the ramp by hands whose owners I could not see, I stood in front of the object upon which leaned dozens of ladders, up which men in white suits scurried with lanterns in their hands—or what I took to be lanterns, the objects in their hands glowed—, lipped over the top rung, and then vanished as into a dormant volcano.

The Head-in-Progress, the Dean of Sedation said, waving at the Head an ivory pipe he produced from deep within his dark robes. This is what I wanted to show you. We knew, I and others, that you would want to form your own opinion on the progress of the project before reporting back to the President. That is what you do, is it not, report back to Ihre Magnifizenz? Well, here's your chance for an exclusive, Herr Abjectus. Take advantage of it. You won't encounter its like again. He patted me on the shoulder and moved me closer toward the Head.

How am I to describe the thing? Obviously I

do not possess the technical knowledge of my prede-cessor, assuming the author of "Final Report to the Intransigence Committee 11/11/__" was my prede-cessor. What do I know of resiliency graphs and rap-ture testing? Of Finite Volume Codes within polar three-dimensional cartesian coordinates? Of tether balloons, which floated above the top of the Head as if it were a fairground beneath a funhouse which held no fun, only fear and a fat man with an axe and a de-mented son? Of PC-LAN and inscription localities? Of anemometry or the flow pyrolysis reactors that hummed with their combustion chambers beneath the Head's chin? All I can do is write what I saw in that vast chamber in my own inadequate words.

Up close, the skin of the Head-in-Progress be-came blurry as bridal satins, but at a distance of two or three feet, one could see scratch marks, like those a child's penknife might make on a school wall, random x's and o's and /'s and \'s and &'s and *'s and #'s and @'s and ^'s and +'s and -'s and ='s and !'s and %'s and $'s. Did these marks form a message, a formula for the scientists to decipher? Several men held magnifying glasses to the surface of the Head, then pulled away to jot something in their notebooks.

The air was thick with the smell of iodine, like the kind my grandmother poured over my scratches after I, chased by shadows, fell over a root in the Cooter Neck woods. You cannot comprehend all of the Head, a voice said. You cannot hold the Head in your hands. But the voice was not coming from my head; it came from speakers in the corners muffled by throwrugs imprinted with scenes of the veldt.

Over and over the voice repeated its sentences, until they were only meaningless chants mingling with the sounds of generators, escaping air pressure, car crashes in the distance, a waterfall.

With the Dean of Platforms I rode a small elevator to the eye. We stepped off the elevator onto the scaffolding, and the Dean, speaking through a voice box at his throat, said: I do not have much longer to work in the University, cancer of the throat, Herr Abjectus, but I am delighted to show you the eye's progress. We have yet to install the C2 Activated Laser Eye Clones. Soon, Herr Abjectus, soon, and then the Head will have the sight granted to all god's creatures, as per Presidential Directive #4958-245893-4589-4854859-48534-535-V2, modified on 12/22/__ to include Presidential Directive 1234567890954321xxx=X1. Until then, I take pride in the work so far, for at my age that is all I can do. My situation is not a pleasant one, I leave with my children baying and biting at my neck, and my wife has forsaken me. I am not, kind sir, an enemy of the President, we've had fine times, the President and I, fine times, fine times together over a bottle or two of Frascati, but that was long ago. I am old, I apologize for the distortion in my voice, the breakdown of my throat.

Kein Problem, no problem, no problem, I said, my usual response when someone speaks a German I cannot comprehend. Then I looked into the hemisphere of the left eye and saw there a host of planets swirling around a sun, but the system was not ours, the planets the wrong shape and dimension, the wrong color and number. In the iris of the other eye

I saw yellow flags fluttering from a white tower in a green sky, and when I looked closer, the landscape became a snow-covered field under a gray sky filled with blackbirds, but this was only the reflection in the eye of the world as seen through the tall windows behind me.

The jaw was a despondent affair, huge and heavy, as if some evil power had imprecated it, so that ringbolts rung with thick hempen ropes had been nailed in strategic places to keep it from sagging.

As we passed the ear, I thought I could hear an old tune, la da da, la da da da da, but I couldn't remember the tune's name. The ear looked like it had been raised from the ocean depths, its edges hung with seaweed and coral.

The whole for some reason reminded me of those afternoons I would spend in the shed at the back of my grandmother's house, where I would slide under lean-tos and dig in the dirt and carve signs on the abandoned furniture, the shed where my grandmother with a rake killed a water moccasin while shouting, Take this and take that! And it reminded me of the Heidelberg Tun in the castle just up the road a ways from Stuttgart.

But what does all this say about the Head-in-Progress? My words cannot describe the nose, the slope of the cheek, the drift westward of the tether balloons. The object was too prodigious in size and form, like the hand of the President caressing my feverish brow, like the University, like the Towers themselves, each Tower a head, each head a Tower, two heads with which to observe the world, like the eyes of a whale, and this Head was only the beginning, perhaps another one was in progress in the other Tower, perhaps once they became operative they would link up, and what then would become of the University?

The Dean of Sedation (of Sedition? I wondered again), stood beside me amidst the febrific activity of the vast Head-in-Progress, and said, Always when I come here to the Head it is snowing, every day it is snowing inside my head.

How can you tell? I asked.

Because the air is so cold, my head is cold.

But what does it mean?

That it must be snowing on the freeways, he said, that the cars are sliding all over the roads, pile-ups everywhere, damage to glass and limb, metal crumpled like paper, my thoughts can't see where they're going, the snow thick, the lights penetrate nothing, drivers and children despair, the thoughts seize up, freeze, mothers give birth to monstrosities that die in the backseats of Fiats.

But what does that mean? I asked again.

I see a sign in the distance, he said.

What does it say?

I can't make it out, he said, the sleet on the glass, the crossings and hatchings in the window, the blood-smeared mirror in the snow like a convulsion of wind, and the moon breaks through the clouds.

But what does it say?

"You are entering another country," he said, and then added, Please be so good as to relay to the President what you have seen, tell her that progress is definitely being made, incremental but significant, that we are behind her, at her side, if only in memory, and we wish her—and you—a pleasant day.

He led me out of the room back into the corridor where an elevator was waiting for me.

I trust you enjoyed your visit, Herr Abjectus, he said.

The elevator doors closed before I could answer him, and I descended to the lower regions.

18. Alone in my Cubicle

My cubicle is cold, cold as the gray afternoon winter sky outside the window.

16.00 hrs.

That is all I can report on what happened to me after the Dean of the late school of the The led me into the Activated Eye and what followed thereafter. It is not enough. The Head alone is worthy of dissertations in a dozen known (and even more unknown) disciplines.

Now that I have written it all down, the central problem remains: the President is nowhere to be found. Not in her office in the H Tower or her office in the S Tower, and according to her secretary not in her penthouse up at the Kräherwald overlooking the city.

Nor is she on an out-of-town trip, for the President would not leave town without an official sendoff. Many times I attended a gathering of journalists, TV people, hangers-on and well-wishers for her departure. First I would put out a general call through the campus mail announcing the President's departure at such and such a time from the Hauptbahnhof—above whose portals reads "...*daß diese Furcht zu irren schon der Irrtum selbst ist,*" that this fear of erring is already itself the error, words by Hegel the President often repeats to me—, and usually this was enough to draw faculty and faculty children and wives to see her off to Bonn or Nürnberg or even as far away as Berlin or Dresden or Prague.

The President prefers, by the way, the old trains, the steam engine ones that roam the tracks like astrodons late into the night beneath my attic window and in their wake leave a light gray streak of smoke against the backdrop of night.

No, she is not on a trip. She is here. I know it. I can sense it in the light coming through the window, in the bones and girders of the Tower, in the wind that is building in the corridors, rumpling awake the sleeping deans, whose coats luff like sheets on a line. She is in the University. I don't know where she is, but she is here somewhere.

I want to rush out of my room into the classrooms, the basement, the tin shed on top of H Tower, the ledge from which I and the gypsies leapt with her into the night sky. Possibilities at every turn, and every place I turn, the President is not there but elsewhere.

I knew how the Towers felt when she was not inside them. At first nothing changes, or a little does—a sudden stiffness, like a jacklighted bunny, inhabits the walls, then a tremor ripples through the corridors and classrooms. Students at that moment are seen to reach for their scarves, to hunker down a bit in their chairs. Professors pause, a vague expression enters their eyes.

They stare out the window at the Katherinenhospital and perhaps ponder for a moment their own bewildering place in the universe.

Or at least this is what I have noticed on those days when she is not here. But after a while, this passes, another symptom manifests itself, as if a voice is saying to them: You must go on, this is your duty as a humble person and good citizen and member of this University whose President wishes you only the best, and expects nothing less. Let the strange energy that is her being pass into you. Let her irrepressibility meld with your susceptibility. Let be imbricate seem.

Then the professors turn back to their students or their paper grading or their letter-of-recommendation writing or their coffee drinking or their ficus plant watering or their sleeping.

Yes, I have seen deans asleep in their offices and broom closets, but only late at night, a time when most people are at home in front of their TVs or tending to necessary domestic matters such as only a countryman can appreciate, and that not always. But these sleeping professors are asleep not from slothfulness, but from dedication and exhaustion. Nor are they the rumored Sleeping or Dead Deans.

I recall one evening as we were leaving work the President and I passed a conference room where seven professors lay with their noses in their beards, and I wanted immediately to run in and rouse them, but the President restrained me with the touch of her hand.

No, Thomas, leave them be. Can't you see they are tired? Who knows what curious problem they have been trying to solve? Perhaps the "weight of incautiousness." Perhaps the problem of "the confidence beyond words," or something even more perplexing like having to find, in these times, a new approach to micromanaging metaphysics.

Perplexities, dear Thomas, she said as we stepped out into the night. Write this down: Appoint a Dean of Perplexities.

For a moment I paused, pretended to be looking at the time table, for we were standing at my bus stop. Should I, I wondered, remind her that such a Dean already existed? No, I thought.

Yes, Ihre Magnifizenz, I said.

Goodnight, Thomas, she said, and made to cross the street, but I shouted, Ihre Magnifizenz! Don't go. I must tell you, I am obliged to and without hesitation, I must hang fire and say the University al … already has a Dean of Perplexities.

She stood still, and for a moment I could not fathom her opaque eyes.

Then, Herr Thomas, she said smiling, I hope you see my point all the more.

Stories of my President—in her absence like vegetables in a children's book they orbit my head!

The President in dazzling light at a dance, gliding across the parquet while men in coats and tails bow as she passes.

The President being shown through splendid rooms in a foreign capital, a small baldheaded man with a gray moustache holding her elbow.

The President in the mountains, alpenstock in hand, looking out over a glacier at the snow-capped mountains spread around her.

But what good are such images. I must try to find her not in an illustrated story book but in real life. It is not a fictive character or a legend who needs to know what is happening in her University; it is the President in all her flesh and fineness and rampageous blood.

Yet alone here in my cubicle, alone in my cell, the blue light of my computer screen humming NO MESSAGES NO MESSAGES, I cannot think where she might be. I know it is urgent that she know what I have seen in the Eye and Head, what I have heard, what rumors flutter through the Towers. Only she could decode what I have been told. Only she could read the subtext hidden like a slice of ham under *Bergkäse*. Only the President, only she, and without her I am a pitiful, worthless personal assistant. Per. ass. is right, I think in my melancholy, my dejection.

I am as foolish as a mouse at the sight of its first mousetrap, as addled as a skeleton, as dumb as a *Schafskopf*. A sad, undermined, forlorn, *Lauscheib, Schurke, Lausbub, Fötzelcheib, Schafseckel*, sorry little fellow, *Taugenichts*, good-for-nothing, worthy of the same, without wit or fortune, without plan or hope. The Towers ditto. The University the same. My job et cetera. What good my pride now, ditto my humility. Nowhere to turn. My President lost. My life …

And so I raged, rage, pitiful wretch who cannot do the job he was hired to do, who can only recall stories about the President, stories that had not made it into *Her Life*, like the story (apocryphal) of the pram that was given to her mother and father when they were very poor by the Minister of Mysterium, and then years later, she noticed my grandmother's last name Bienenkopf was the same as the Minister and thus, putting two and two and two together, offered me a job on the spot, while the bright red Pegasus above the lube bay doors neighed in the Arkansas sun.

The story of her first encounter with water, and what the water said when it saw her magnificent, magisterial face. The story of light, of wind, of snow, and how she rose on the wings of their stories to her position in the Towers today. The story of…

But what good are these fictions? What good do they do her or me?

I didn't know what to do.

I'm finished, I thought. *Kaputt.*

At which point the telephone on my desk hunkered down a little deeper in its cradle, trembled for a moment, and then loudly, violently began to ring.

19. Dunkelbach

Abjectus, I said into the receiver.

Dunkelbach, the voice at the other end replied.

Dunkelbach? I asked. The Merrittean? What did *he* want with *me*?

The same, he said. On 4aHT.

What may I do for you, Herr Dunkelbach? I'm afraid I'm quite busy at the moment with work for the President. Itineraries to confirm, speeches to revise, reports to file. Much work for me today, Herr Dunkelbach.

It's like a hive, if you want to know the truth, I added without thinking, slipping into my confidential mode, which I noticed pleased the staff. A busy busy hive, working for the President. But of course, what I do is not absolutely essential. The President does not need my input or labors. Yes, a busy hive, but one I am happy to have tumbled into.

When I stopped my chatter, I thought I could hear in the background, over Dunkelbach's breathing, "Little One" from Miles Davis's *ESP*. Then at once I realized that the music was coming from another line, not from Dunkelbach's. I tried to follow through the music into the room itself, where, for all I knew, the President had been kidnapped by some unyielding member of the opposition party. Or perhaps she was sipping Frascati at some colleague's house, feet propped up after a long day's work, a moment of well-earned relaxation for her indefatigable Magnifizenz. I had no way of confirming any of these scenarios, but something told me that, as surely as my name was Abjectus, the latter was not the case.

An urgent matter, Dunkelbach said.

I beg your pardon?

About the President, he said. Come down.

Even though I could no longer hear the music, I was having a hard time understanding the professor.

Where?

Here.

But Herr Dunkelbach, I said, the President...

We need to talk.

In his voice, I could detect no threat and, oddly, no fear.

A few moments later I was standing before a lanky figure, bedecked in what I've learned were a C3's traditional, mouse-gray robes. On each wrist he wore a large moon-faced watch, no doubt in honor of one of A. Merritt's most famous books. Framed on his cream-colored walls were covers from the early 1950s Avon paperbacks of his speciality's science fiction.

Always so sad, Herr Abjectus, he said, motioning me into a chair. Is anything troubling you? Can't you say what it is? Homesick, perhaps, for your homeland's great open spaces? Confused by the Swabians?

It's easier for those who were born here, dear Herr Assistant, than it is for you, and you have my deepest sympathy and understanding.

Which I welcome with the humblest and most open arms, I said, taking the straight-backed wooden chair he had offered. But you said something over the phone about the President.

Dunkelbach pushed his silver glasses up his nose, shifted in his chair his middle-aged frame, and nodded his head.

What did this curious figure want from me? He wasn't even a dean. What possibly could he tell me? But I had come because I didn't know what else to do. And perhaps he would inadvertently reveal information that would lead me to the President.

He tapped a pen firmly on the desk, then on his gold eyetooth, leaned toward me, and said, I've heard you've had a busy day.

Yes, I said, quite busy, and much left for me to do. Who told you?

Dunkelbach, as his glasses slipped down his nose, spread his arms wide. For a moment he looked like some giant fantastic insect from one of his author's novels.

Well, sir, he said conspiratorially, everyone talks, and for better or worse I have ears, and my ears tell me that you are having a very busy day, a most fatiguing day, one that has left you and—how shall I say this— us, somewhat bereft. For you, like I, like the rest of us, are at present unaware of the President's whereabouts.

I raised my hand to interrupt him, but he went on.

I know, he said, I'm only a measly C3 professor with an obscure specialty, but I am also the only figure in this plant, I mean planet, I mean University you can t-t-t-t-t-trust.

I noted his stutter and noted he noted my noting it.

It's true, though you and I both wish it were not. Have you ever wondered why it was you the President hired?

Yes, I said, occasionally the thought has entered my mind.

Ignoring my sarcasm, he said, And so have I wondered why she hired me. But unlike you I have discovered why.

He paused in order, I assume, to see my response, but I merely smiled at him and said, Excellent, Herr Dunkelbach, I am sure the President will be glad to learn that you have achieved your epiphany.

Here, he said, and handed me a copy of *The Moon Pool*. Look at Chapter Twenty-Eight, "In the Lair of the Dweller," and then you'll understand.

I opened the old, flaky thing, and read its standard beginning: "It is with marked hesitation that I begin this chapter, because in it I must deal with an experience so contrary to every known law of physics as to seem impossible." The only thing missing was the exclamation mark. The rest I remember but vaguely—a tale about increasingly radiant and orgastic epiphanies as our narrator descended deeper into rock.

I wondered what any of this had to do with the President, and I wondered how anyone could be allowed to teach such drivel, much less specialize in it? Was Dunkelbach totally mad, or was he perceptive beyond my ability to understand? Was he a genius, a fool, a weird fiction created by himself, or simply a lowly C3 who had information that would lead me to the President?

Regardless, I could read no more, and finally I looked up and saw the expectancy in Dunkelbach's face that could be nothing other than devotion to and support of the President. I could not then doubt him. He loved the President as much as I.

He rose from his chair and I from mine, and we met in the middle of the room and embraced.

Two grown men, he said over and over, two grown men.

His thin arms wrapped me into them, wrapped themselves into me, and me into his robes, and, oddly, I welcomed him.

One is one, I thought he breathed into my ear. One is one—and a brief tintinnabulation went off in my head.

Then he said, You noticed my limp.

Yes, yes, I nodded, though in truth I had not.

Let me tell you a story, he said, and hugged me even deeper into his bony warmth. Let me tell you a tale, now that you know why I was hired, now that you have surmised an analysis equal to the revelation I felt one day in the hallways of 11ST.

Okay, I said.

Throughout what he next said, we remained in each other's arms, his breath warm against my ear, his chin, for such a small head, heavier on my shoulder than I had expected.

Once, he said, I was coming out of the office of a friend of mine on S Tower's 11th floor, i.e., 11ST, a floor you must know well yourself. How I admire and envy you, Herr Abjectus! But to continue: As I walked down the corridor, the gray light pouring in through the west window, I saw the President walking toward me, her body trailing light behind it—like Dylan Thomas's windfall light, eh? Suddenly, I cannot say what exactly overcame me, my limp became more prominent, my stutter more unmanageable. When we met, the President and I, in the center of the hall, I was prepared to nod as best I could and then hurry past. Very few C3s, you know of course, are ever seen on 11ST, fewer I would say, though I cannot offer here any firm evidence to support it, than C3s on 11HT. I leave gladly that old argument to scholars with more breadth than I have, my specialty a rather obscure corner of the scholarly cosmos. But once again to continue: Wearing the cloak of inconspicuousness, as it were, around me, I prepared to rush past her, when she said, with a musical lilt that I shall never forget: I see, Herr Dunkelbach, that your limp is more pronounced. Yes, yes, I said, bowing before her and stepping back at the same time, yes, it is, Ihre Magnifizenz. Sports? she asked. Yes, I confessed. Ah, dear Herr Dunkelbach, don't tell me you bought whole hog into that old macho canard "Sports builds character." And then she laughed heartily for several moments—I of course laughed with her—, patted me on the back and walked away.

Dunkelbach's lips pulled away from my neck. We held each other at arm's length, excited by our long embrace.

I have something to show you, he said. Something that might be of vital importance.

Then you must show it to me without delay, I said.

He rushed to a filing cabinet beside a ficus tree, opened the top shelf and extracted three ordinary manilla folders.

Within each of these folders, he said, is a report I have filed on subversives determined to bring down the President. I want you to read them.

The firm tone of his voice told me I should do as he said, but in order to be one hundred percent certain I asked, Do you think one of these groups might be behind the President's disappearance?

I believe that's a possibility, he said.

I picked up the folders, strangely light, and sat down in the wooden chair. The weather outside had not changed—snow, gray, freezing. I didn't know whether it was four or five or eight in the evening, and I didn't know what I was about to learn, what surprises awaited me. But I had to read these folders if I was going to help the President who, only a short time ago, I had, if only for a moment, begun to doubt. Was I to end up like my predecessor on my back on a glass table with my kneecaps about to be shattered, I had wondered. No. I was going to read about the President's enemies and try to understand their mysteries and motivations, their delusions and dreams.

I opened the first folder.

20. The Internecine Wars

"... of a strange mineral that glowed and shifted in a liquid light. A foot or two away stood something like the standee of a compass, bearing like it a cradled dial under whose crystal ran concentric rings of prisoned, lambent vapours, faintly blue. From the edge of the dial jutted a little shelf of crystal, a keyboard, in which were cut eight small cups about to be fingered." All of which sounded more Merritt to me than Dunkelbach.

But after a while the text settled down to a steady march of revelations about the IWC III, i.e. the Third Internecine War Council, about which I learned, by sifting and sorting Dunkelbach's hints and feints at meanings that I could only partially fathom, the following: that the above-mentioned keyboard belonged in the Music Room of 7.3aST, an area I was not familiar with, and it was in this room where the conspirators met.

For conspirators they were. No names were assigned to these hooded figures, only letters; thus I, too, can only refer to them as Herr A or Herr B.

Herr D: "Herr Abjectus, heh, heh, or shall we call him Herr Undsoweiter, is a cornered pawn, forget about him." And here in Dunkelbach's office on 4aST, with the little light refusing to fade from view the reflected stare of S Tower across the way, how could I fail to concur?

Still, I read on. And learned that the IWC III had plans to replace the President. They wanted the Faculty Senate to file Form # (*_)(*_)(*&*&*&20 For Immediate Postponement. They wanted to bypass the President, Ihre Magnifizenz, and elect a new Chancellor. Certain memories should be excised from the consciousness of the Towers. Things must be said that cannot ever beyond this room be allowed forth. They wanted to wait it out, they wanted immediate action, they wanted one single man, only one man, that is all it would take, to take care of the President.

The letters splashed over me, took me into their undertow. Rumor chased fact, and fact rumor, like a dog chasing its own tail. Herr R: "We eat when we are hungry, when we are hungry we eat." Herr X: "A coin rubbed as a fine as a razor blade, strategically placed, can do enormous devastation. Enough to make her think the Russians were here." Herr E: "Having refrained for some years from involving myself with the inner workings of the University, I have concluded that if power makes right, then power sets us free." Herr P: "I do not doubt it." Herr U: "Dark as these times are." Herr K: "Of course."

Against this undertow I struggled, tried to regain the surface, but again and again was pulled down into the vortex of whispers, rantings, threats of maiming and assassination. When such power locates itself in one room, one aggregate or individual..., but the rest of my thought I could not formulate.

While I read, Dunkelbach paced his office, from the wall with the Merritt covers, to the wall with the window, to the wall with the mirror door (a broom or clothes closet, I assumed), to the wall with the front door; from the corner with his desk, to the corner with the ficus plant (its leaves pale and still), to a point behind my head, where he would pause for a moment, put his hand on my shoulder, lean over, breathe in my ear, and say, Yes, yes, somewhere in there, it's somewhere in there, then begin again his pacing.

Herr F: "Of course it doesn't matter finally the method, as long as it is we who are elevated. It is we who should be in charge of the Towers, assuming that anyone, any committee can be in charge of such an entity, such an institution with its long, checkered, legend-filled, baroque and byzantine, heroic, hoary, exemplary past, such a singular force on the mind of the State. But, gentlemen, in no way should it be the President, whose reign is a farrago of missteps and misery." Herr V: "Consensus." Herr C: "Consensus and sanguinary dreams."

I closed the folder, my mind wearied from a conspiracy deeper than I ever thought possible.

Dunkelbach towered over me.

What did you find?

Nothing that would lead us to the President, I said. Only the ravings of professors I cannot understand. What is it supposed to mean, all this animosity toward the President?

Power, Dunkelbach said, power and contingencies. These are the hungry ones who will feed on anything to achieve their unspeakable goal.

I handed him Folder A, and he continued:

Listen carefully, Abjectus. No one is kidding here. They wish her dead, at the least. You understand me?

I nodded.

Good. Otherwise there's no hope of our finding the President. Have you ever thought how many other couples, if I may be so bold, are at this same moment searching for clues to her whereabouts? How many of them are there, do you think, who think the same as you and I? A dozen? Less? Three? One? No one? Yes? Yes. No one, Herr Abjectus, no one except you and I still trust Ihre Magnifizenz. Can you fathom the possible consequences? Well, that's what I've been doing the past fifteen months. Yes, my reports began fifteen months ago, in a time of turmoil at the University, long before your arrival. The President had given her Unification speech, when protestors began to storm the podium, and she, rather than stand up and fight, simply said into the microphone, "Well, dear rowdies. If you want the bloody thing so much, then take it," flipped the mike dead, and left the stage. The rowdies, as she politely called the Deans who resembled butchers whose daughters have all just been raped and tossed into the ditches at the sides of a country road—these rowdies, as I was saying, slowed in their tracks, whuffled about for a moment in the dust, then stumbled back to their seats. After some five minutes of mumbling, the audience got up and left. The next day the paper had spread the scandal over the front page and the President was in hiding. Yes, this, or something similar, has happened before. Look for the forthcoming *Dunkelbach's Version*, to be followed a year later by *Her Memoirs*. If my memory is not mistaken, which, like most things in the universe, it has every right to be, then the President as I speak is likely in grave danger. And somewhere in these folders may lie the answer. You hold it in your hands. Read the other two. The internecinaries, as I like to call them, aren't the only group committed to overthrowing the President. No, sir. Not by a long shot. There's still B and C to consider, and who knows how many untold number of others I've yet to catalogue.

Dunkelbach seemed to drift off for a moment, and I perhaps with him. The room's walls closed in on me, the air was thick and warm. Was my sudden langour due to my not believing a word Dunkelbach was saying? And yet if I accepted that, what hope then for the President or the University?

The President, Dunkelbach continued, has plans no one else has. And this is what scares them, let me say it loud and clear. It is these plans, or rather not the plans, but the fact that she is willing to plan that unnerves them. Madness, Herr Abjectus, madness. Make a note. And read on, for her sake, my friend, read on. It is still snowing. I don't expect it to stop tonight. I've read all the documents and books written since 1966 by the Deans of Winds and Weather. Not that I, like so many of my colleagues expect an appointment with or from the President. Never would I expect such a thing. Our one meeting in the hall, surely that is enough for a lifetime. Don't the deans realize how privileged they are? But do carry on, do carry on. B and C still to come, each as subversive as A, but each their own strange country.

The framed book jackets on the wall shimmered for a moment, and I felt a sudden coldness throughout my limbs.

What was it?

Dunkelbach, standing now at the window, appeared unaffected.

I straightened my cuffs, buttoned my wool coat, then pulled out the next folder.

21. DFMW

The Towers seemed to sway, when I spread Folder B open on my lap and began to read about the DFMW.

DFMW? What could that mean? Dunkelbach's report on this group did not immediately reveal the answer. My eyes swam over and through seas that were beyond anything resembling Merritt. I wondered if Dunkelbach himself fathomed more than a thimbleful of what he had recorded. Children before some strange, possibly dangerous toy just opened at Christmas cannot decide if they'd rather laugh or cry. This is how I felt reading this report.

I was a miner clambering down an unsteady ladder nailed higgledy-piggledy into the rock, while a pool of coal dust beneath me awaited like a bottomless well.

I could make little sense of the document, except that throughout it all swam, shark-like, a riveting misogyny. Was this, I wondered, the "one solid, but still crescentic centre" my grandmother told me Melville spoke of?

It began: "May she fold up within herself like slabs of meat in a fat sandwich. May she be siphoned into her own throat, and may her throat then take wing and wrap itself around Kaiser Wilhelm astride his bronze horse, like Peter the Great, on the Schlossplatz. All because this abomination, this simulacrum of femininity has been set free to make us into that which we were never meant to be, i.e., pages poised outside her door, ever ready at her behest to spring forth into battle. May she be set upon by cancer cells. May she be ravaged by them. May she choke on a piece of toast. For Hate's sake, do all these things we wish, and our last professorial breaths we spit at Ihre Magnifizenz, who disallows us a Dean of Circumferences when we most need one, who conflates when we least expect it, who has broken covenant incalculable times, who rages when slighted which is often, who plays with her prey in order to torture it, who fears her enemies for good reason."

And ended: "We will feast on her flesh, for if there were a god he would not have made us suffer her."

Then I heard the chant, yes, *heard* it before I comprehended the printed text, as if the voice behind the words poured through the open space between me and the page, between me and the words, and through the upside-down v in the W, through the bracket in the F, a wind swirled down the corridors of the University, into the lecture rooms, the classrooms, offices and closets.

I clutched tight the folder, and bowed my head under the weight of the chant:

DFMW!
DFMW!
DIE FRAU MUSS WEG!
DIE FRAU MUSS WEG!
THE WOMAN MUST LEAVE!
DIE FRAU MUSS WEG!
DIE FRAU MUSS WEG!

How, I wondered, could one woman, especially one as dear as Ihre Magnifizenz, be the object of so much hatred?

Yes, Dunkelbach interrupted my thoughts to say, don't we most want what most fellows desire? A *Traumfrau*? And isn't that what the DFMW most fear, the woman of their dreams? Madness, Herr Abjectus, madness and jealousy. How to arrest it? I don't know. Perhaps these are the ones who have her now? I can't say, I simply can't say. Read on, Herr Assistant, read on.

I closed Folder B with a sense of befuddled finality. Considerably more informed, I was nonetheless no less uncertain about the fate of the President than I was before. Had she been kidnapped by the madmen in A or B? Was there a code buried in Dunkelbach's reports, a code he himself did not know, that once cracked would show us where the President was being kept? Madness, yes, Dunkelbach was right about that. But what was it we were looking for exactly? They hated the President. They wished to bend her, to break and overthrow her. But what were their methods, what their plans?

Dunkelbach, I said, what is it...

But when I looked up, Dunkelbach was no longer there.

22. Alone in Dunkelbach's Office

I rushed after him, but down the long, empty corridor cast in a spectral haze, I saw no Dunkelbach, no deans, no one.

Back inside his office I stood before the mirrored door and observed there Herr Abjectus. He wore his dark-gray wool suit, his tie (marigolds against a ruby-red background), his Arkansas boots (polished, but snow-stained), his gray wool socks, a haggard face.

If only I could get to the President! I had learned more in the past few hours about the secret maneuverings of numerous professors and deans than I had during the entire first semester of my tenure. A Fafner's load of treasure I could give her. If only I could! If only I could let her know what I had learned!

But the all-too-familiar figure in the mirror offered me no answer. I had done my job, filed my reports, written speeches, delivered messages in envelopes sealed with her signature, respected her, admired her—dare I say it?—, adored her. If it hadn't been for Dunkelbach, I might have begun to truly question my devotion to the President. If it were only I who stayed faithful to Ihre Magnifizenz, I do not think I could trust myself. I am not, after all, am I, merely her dog. And even dogs sometimes rebel.

No, I was no dog, no slavish pup or, for that matter, pet of Schopenhauer, but I had will and my will said I could if I so desired doubt the President *in parte* but not *in toto caelo*. And why should I? Other than the fact that the President was nowhere to be found, that she was likely in grave danger at the moment or at least in the near future (a safe assumption on the basis of Dunkelbach's reports and what I myself had detected, uncovered, gleaned in my recent encounters with the Dean of Archives, the Dean of Conflation, the Dean of Sedation, my predecessor's or predecessors' reports to committees), and that when she most needed me I was unable to go to her aid.

Dunkelbach had departed, but why? Had he gone to the WC, trotted off a moment on the sly so as not to disturb my reading? Or had something more dire occurred? Had he, too, been kidnapped? Was I next? Were the three of us, Dunkelbach, the President and I, about to lose our jobs, our reputations, our lives?

What else could I do after such tortuous musings but turn back to Dunkelbach's final report, Folder C.

Though the shortest of them all, it dragged on and on, and dragged me down with it. One moment I thought I was reading about the Dean of Mountain Climbing, the next about the Dean of Straws and Magnitude. One minute I'm flotsam on the sea, the next a time bomb in a Petersburg bourgeois household. The group had, as best I could assess, no name.

What name would fit an organization that wanted the University to change its constitution to its death certificate, that is, that all activities within the Towers must desist over a period not to exceed one year and not sooner than next year? This is what they wanted: for the University to devour itself, to become its own worst enemy, to rid itself of itself.

Did they feel all powerful, this group? Is that why they so blithely gave their names, or was there a deception in this openness? The Dean of Music was amongst these conspirators, as well as the Dean of Forgone Conclusions, the Dean of Pertinacity, the Dean of Nightclothes, the Dean of Neuroscience, the Dean of Worship, the Dean of Oncology, the Dean of Zoos, the Dean of Mercurial Talents (even he!), the Dean of Rubberstamping and Safety Zones.

Many of these deans I knew personally, and the last one was one of the President's most trusted confidantes. If the President had a confidante, it wasn't I but the Dean of Rubberstamping and Safety Zones, who met with her often for asparagus soup and wine in various local *Stuben*. So the deception went even this far! Where did it end?

Ah, Ihre Magnifizenz, I moaned out loud, tossing the filthy thing at my feet.

And where was Dunkelbach?

23. The Inner Chambers

The elevators were unnaturally slow. I thought they would never come to take me back to the President's office (surely she would have come back by now, surely all the folders were merely Dunkelbach's mad fantasies), that the hall would fade into the winter darkness that still had yet to arrive.

I paced back and forth in front of the glistening metal doors. Would winter ever bring on its night and release me back into the snow whence I had come, where I would make my way once more to the 42 bus stop, climb on the bus thick with bulky, fur-coated bodies, with Germans, Austrians, Lebanese, Turks, bringing home their suppers in stuffed, steaming grocery bags, and I would clutch as always a handhold for support, and sway back and forth until the driver announced, in his cigarette-coarsened voice, that I had arrived at Landhausstraße 43, and the door would open when I pressed the soft, white button (*Tür öffnen*) attached to a pole, then gripping firmly the bars, I descend onto the iced sidewalk, noting the message scarred thereon from the weight of thousands of feet, as incomprehensible as ever, and then one careful step at a time make my way uphill to Werfmershalde 12, climb the stairs to my attic apartment, where I lay down my backpack, my briefcase, my overcoat, and stand at the window and stare out at the lights of the city, what I could see of them, and the Towers and all they contained would be lost in the haze and clouds and snow.

When finally the middle elevator came, its bell ringing as brightly as a surprised wind chime and the arrow pointing upward flashed white, the doors did not open immediately. They appeared to hesitate, pause. I waited, but still they did not open.

And then it was as if I could hear them thinking, the elevators, could hear them whispering to one another: Should we let him in? Is it too early? Is it too late? What wishes to reside in us? Should we let it in? Are these corridors compulsory? What are the two elements? Heaviness and darkness? He wishes to go up? Why not down?

Were these the voices of the elevators, or was I hearing the voices of the Deans of Engineering and Business or the Dean of Carnivals and Culture, a position eliminated long ago? Or was it my own forlorn thoughts lost in the University's maze?

I tilted my tired head against the metal doors, but the voices only grew louder. They spoke of the wind, of the President; they spoke of what came next and what came after but never of now; they spoke of the winter, of the Head and the Activated Eye and of the Gestation Chamber. They asked, Is he one of us or one of them? Well, why not let him in then?

The elevator door opened with an audible sigh.

I stepped in, pressed 11, and waited.

The door shut.

The elevator did not move.

Then, slowly, grudgingly, it did, and with each floor we passed, each blink of the red numbers above the door, my spirits grew stronger and stronger. Soon, I knew, I would see the President.

I got off on the 11th floor and hurried to her office. But this time the secretary was not in the outer office, and I walked straight and without hesitation to the door marked Ihre Magnifizenz.

For a moment I held my fist raised before it, then decided not even to knock, just pushed open the door with my shoulder and, stumbling across the threshold, rushed headlong in.

The President looked up from behind her desk, then quickly shuffled the papers in front of her into a pile, slipped them into a loose manilla folder, and the folder into a briefcase, which she promptly locked.

My goodness, Thomas, she said. What in the world are you doing here, and at this time of day?

Nothing in her office, her private chambers, had changed. She rose from her black desk (that formed a meniscular moon around her), like an administrator who had put in a long day, and now at the end of the day is surprisingly interrupted by an overly eager young assistant.

My body was filled with an urgency to help her, but everything about her and the room's sameness belied my need. The ficus plant, the podium, the dark lake of her table we had so often worked around, the refrigerator in which I had already set this morning, all in a row, seven bottles of Frascati—all these things: her bookshelves not too crowded, as if at any time she could move from H Tower to S Tower, and containing titles such as *Der Gehülfe* (my gift on her fiftieth birthday, which did not, her fiftieth, go unnoticed by the University at large), Wellek and Warren's *Theory of Literature* (an old favorite of mine as well), multiple copies of her own distinguished publications including her bestselling *Der Weg zum Erfolg* (*The Way to Success*, translated into French—less successfully—as *Madame Ministry*), and, not surprisingly, a copy of my grandmother's novel; all these things down to the deep blue carpet that my feet sponged into, down to its finest thread—, all these things, as I said, were as they ever were, commanding in their solidity and placidity, attuned to the President's presence, her wishes, her moves.

As she walked toward me, her head cocked questioningly to one side, the dark, massive clouds behind her pressed their thick foreheads, like tired giants, against the windowpane.

"Ihre Magnifizenz!" I shouted. "You are in grave danger! Where have you been?!"

"But, Thomas," she said, freezing in the center of the room, "I have been here all along. Surely there has been some mistake."

At which point—

At which point—

And it is beyond this point I wish to go no further. How can I replay what happened next? How can I even think of reliving it? It is when I recall it that I

most despair of completing my report to the committee, whom I see dressed in their robes around a golden
conference table, awaiting with bated breaths my next
chapter. Even this is not sufficient to make me eager to
continue. Had I known that I would ever be required
to write what I am about to, I would have never, I am
sure, allowed myself to be spirited out of my homeland
like some silly school girl enamored of that which can,
and probably will, most do her harm, into this strange
country, this strange snow-locked university, where
even my best efforts were not good enough. I do not,
no, indeed, do not, sirs, gentle deans of the Committee,
my President, want to write what I am about to write.
But replay it all I must, if my report is to be filed and
the story of what happened next to the President be
told, and so replay it I shall.

At which point Dunkelbach jumped out from behind the secretary's desk, where he must have been hiding all this time, like some future Russian prince turned
bolshevik steeling himself for his ultimate subversive
act, pushed himself from the desk with his left hand,
as if he were jumping side-saddle onto a horse, landed
with a loud thump on the threshold between the outer
(Secretary's) office and the inner (the President's) chambers, tapped, as if for luck, his one gold tooth, pushed
his silvery frames up his nose, shook for a moment like
a wet dog, except his C3, mouse-gray robes seemed to
be shedding light rather than water—while all this time
the President and I stared in wonder and amazement...

At which point—

At which point, Dunkelbach pulled a gun from
his robes and shot her.

24. Death

I leaned over her dying form, unable to understand fully what was happening. Dunkelbach had… he had… Dunkelbach had shot the President. Where had he gone? But all my attention was on the President, and I watched in dismay the blood spread wine-red through her charcoal-gray wool suit. At first in a trickle, then in a rush the blood came out of her heart.

As I turned my head from the fatal wound, an image of Dunkelbach appeared in my mind's eye, a blurred image of his robes fluttering around him as he spun away from the threshold of the inner chambers, his face hidden from view by his upthrust forearm like some fantastic, comic-book villain, and then the image vanished into the University's dark, labyrinthine spaces.

The President looked up at me, but in the pools of her opaque eyes I could see there no pain or joy, only an odd implacability; pools without dimension or depth. No longer were they the eyes whose blueness I could hear say, You are welcome to gaze into me, Herr Thomas, but do not take too much notice or attempt to make a scene over me. I am only your President. Though I can do much, and have, I cannot do everything. We have the rest of our lives to speak to one another. Do not rush. Take your time. Calm down. There, Herr Thomas, now you can speak.

No, those eyes were gone, and on their surface now floated only my own terrified face.

Ihre Magnifizenz, I managed to say, but my words only barely came out of my mouth. I could hardly speak, and if I tried again, I knew I would weep.

I saw her try to rise from the deep blue carpet, but then she collapsed back onto it. Was she trying to tell me something? Was there something, some final word, she wished to impart to me, her personal assistant these past several months?

Her lips trembled then, and I bowed my face toward them.

Thomas, she said in a voice free from any mask, you must not despair. The past and the future circle about us always. Listen to me. Come closer. What was the University before it was the University? Don't you see, Thomas? Life sketches more marvelously than we ever could.

She paused and I saw, round her pallid brow, ringlets of her hair deceptively play, as if she were some character in a Swiss novel. Then she continued.

Now we know more, now less, but always we think we know when we do not. Forgive me. I can only suggest that which is within me. I detect no sign of dissolution, even though I know my body is leaving me. For a time, our bodies stay here for us, then they depart. But does that say anything? What soul-force compels me to speak beyond my end? Give yourself, Herr Assistant, a lot of rest. That's my best advice. I remain at the edge, the current shall leave me alone a while longer. Don't let yourself be so easily seduced. Your susceptibility to the voices of others, yes, even to my enemies', I always found the most troubling aspect of your character. Many a time I wondered if I should let you go. Was I, I wondered, even doing you a favor by letting you remain in my employ in such a treacherous university? But everywhere is the same, dear Thomas. The trees know this and that is why they travel only in their dreams. I am Vogel Selbsterkenntnis, remember. The clouds know why they crowd to the window. On the Neckar I see a tugboat, and above a vineyard on a hill, between a biplane and a zeppelin, a dark gray balloon rises into an azure sky. What land do you think I will arrive in next?

Suddenly she clutched my coat lapels and brought me down even closer to her death. Listen very carefully, my little one. Are you listening? Good.

Her eyes closed, but almost at the precise moment they closed, they opened wide again, and she continued as if she had never been away, as if all that she had said before were mere prelude or child's play in the face of what she was now saying.

I want to take you into my heart, she said. I want to take you into this winter, but I cannot, except in words. Still, Herr Little One, you must listen to the wind that is in the winter, the winter in the wind. The Towers arise out of the snow, and the snow in turn sometimes arises from the Towers. You have the makings of a conduit for dreams, but don't let your good nature be taken for granted. In the University it is always winter. Always these giants have trembled outside the window, these old giants who want only to rest their heavy heads in my lap. But you will see, Herr Thomas, if you will only wait, snowdrops pushing up their little white blossoms at the feet of the birches. What lies behind the clouds? Can you look into them and see what lies beyond? Is that a Tower you see? What flag flies there? Gold, red-gold, black-gold, or the flag of some other as yet to be discovered country, where the natives do not dream ever in red, but always and only in blue, and the sky and wind know their wishes? Or are those our two Towers, Humanities and Sciences, swaying outside ourselves while we drift on our daily courses in the rude stream within? Or are there three Towers you see, Thomas, there, beyond the snow? Look closely, closer. Heavy on the eyelids of the sleeper falls the snow in thick, clumpy flakes that hang big on every branch, bend every twig, and mute the world around it. Can you still hear me, dear Herr Kleinergehülfe? Are you still here?

I nodded and listened on in wonder at her words.

Perhaps you are the only one who understood what it was I wanted to accomplish. Yes, I am sure of it. No one but you understood the basis upon which rested my daily agenda, directive, meeting, constitutional alteration, reassignment of schools, deans, professors, committees, rooms, desks, podiums, chalk trays, Mensa menus, high teas. You alone, Thomas, have understood me. No, dear Thomas, do not shake your silly little head, do not weep over the death of the President. Think of all the Presidents who came before me. Can you name even one? It all passes before you know it and when you know it, it's too late. I am not ready to die, despite all that I have accomplished, all that I have said. There is more, and there will be more. That I promise you. Can it have happened that once I, a traveller, came to your strange land and there espied you at a distance atop a wooden Coca-cola rack beneath the red sign of Pegasus? Stranger rumors about the two of us abound. Thomas, I want to take you completely into my confidence, completely into my heart. You cannot choose a feeling. You can only choose an action. This is one of the things I have discovered during my terms as President of the University of the Two Towers. I wish only to tell you the truth. Once upon a time I lived in a small, over-heated room. Against the wall at the end, for the room was more of a boxcar than a room, were a desk beneath a window and a lamp on a small, white, circular nightstand. Against the side walls were an old sofa thick with dust and an ironing board. Against the front wall were a light switch and a door with three locks. The first lock used a key, the second lock a combination, and the third lock no one knew how to open but I and an old woman, my landlady. Its secret was revealed to me by her before she passed away. She used to come to my room and tell me strange stories and accuse me of traducing her, which I never did. Still, she carried on. "Why is it you lie about me? What harm did I ever do you? Haven't I told you the secret of the third lock, so why do you tell lies about me? All the things you

137

say you have discovered, those are all lies. I am only a landlady! Nothing more, nothing less. And I am old. I am older than you can ever guess. What you are I do not know, but of me I can say I am only an old landlady. Go, go away now. I have nothing more to say to you." I listened to her ravings week after week, but I could not stop her. Finally, one day, she died, and in her will she left me her house and modest fortune. Herr Thomas, closer, come closer still. I want to feel your breath on my face. Thank you. You were always a clever pup, if possessed, albeit, of only a, how shall I say, modest fortitude. Yes, you've been quite indispensable to me, even if I must admit my weakness for your sort. Your childish chatter often amused me. But, Herr Kleinchen, for too long have you thought of me as a figure from fantasy, a queen in a Tower, when all along I have only been and only always will be your altogether ordinary Ihre Magnifizenz. But this isn't a fairy tale, Thomas; this is real blood that flows out of my body, not some jelly out of a movie actor, not the blood of some mythic heroine. Real blood, Herr Thomas. Touch it, put your finger gently into it, then bring your fingers to your open lips. This is me you are tasting, Thomas, *ich*, my and only my blood. Perhaps this is all I've been trying to say.

Then the President's eyes closed, her body shuddered, as if her inmost soul had suddenly been gripped and squeezed by a huge hand, and all over her skin turned yellow—the tips of her fingers, her eyelids, her lips.

Ihre Magnifizenz was dead.

25. The Official Report

The Official Report had it different.

The Official Report did not mention me or Dunkelbach or her final words. That is to say, they mentioned me in passing (fourth paragraph of a sidebar on page 18 of the special issue of *Der Turm* containing the Official Report), and her final words were, officially, "Perhaps this is the best thing"—with the "this" left entirely unspecified.

The Official Report, as it was usually called (or abbreviated to OFF or TOR), officially was called Preliminary Official Report on the Assassination of the President, but no matter its name it bore no relation to reality.

The Official Report came off the press with surprising promptness on the afternoon of the next day, or at least what I thought to be the next day, I can't be sure, for they kept me locked in a small cell of the University and asked me questions, these curious deans I had never seen before, who kept their faces behind masks, and wore white robes over their traditional gray ones.

I told them about Dunkelbach's keeping me occupied over three folders marked A, B, and C, each purporting to be a report filed by Dunkelbach, a lowly *Wissenschaftlicher Assistent*, but perhaps were mere diversions to keep me from seeing his true design: the assassination of the President. I told them about what was in the folders, about the DFMW [*Die Frau Muss Weg*], about the IWC III [Third Internecine War Council], about the black poodle and the Head-in-Progress, about the radical metaphysics of Folder C. I then proceeded to implicate the President's secretary in the conspiracy (Why wasn't she there when the President was assassinated? Why didn't she let me into the inner chambers when I arrived on time for a scheduled appointment, assuming the agenda I saw had not been faked?), and then to implicate the deans of some 62 schools, as well as members of some 29 sundry committees.

My interrogators stared blankly behind their masks at me.

My interrogators flipped open their tape recorders and changed the cassettes.

My interrogators did not believe me.

So I told them the story again, adding only a few newly recalled images (Dunkelbach pausing at the window as though he had just seen something out there, then backing away with a start, and beginning his pacing once again while I read from Folder B; the President smiling, as if to herself, over a cup of hot tea; the ten *Elstern*, i.e., Pica pica, I thought I saw ruffling their wings in a snow-laden fir tree), but I always kept to the central, primary truth, *nämlich*, that

Dunkelbach had shot the President.

My interrogators pulled their robes tighter about their bodies.

My interrogators still did not believe me.

What happened next, they asked, what happened next what happened next what happened next what happened next—over and over, until I didn't know myself what happened next, and I may have begun, after hours of their questioning me from their golden dais while I sat below them in the same wooden chair (by chance or by design, I couldn't help but wonder) that I had sat in in Dunkelbach's office, may have begun, as I said, to sift and sort the scenes, move them about here and there within narrative's carnival flow. Various random disclosures referring to various periods of time hitherto having more or less required that I set down their occurrences in order, now became "irregularly given," as the old Customs House inspector once wrote. I may have strayed, I may have inflected a scene or two, but I did not, never once did I, nor ever once will I, not come back to the simple core fact of Dunkelbach's killing the President.

Down to the last detail, down to the last gleam of light that barred his mad eye as he spun away from the threshold—I gave them my story of the assassination of the President, but I do not think they ever believed me, and to this day I do not know if they do.

They kept me for three days in a tiny cell with a concrete floor and padded walls and no window, only a blanket and plastic chair in which, on the first day, I refused to sit. At least I think it was three days; occasionally I covered myself with the blanket and slept, and sometimes my sleep was so deep that I couldn't recall if I'd just slept two hours or fourteen.

On the second day I was given a copy of the Official Report. It spoke of "the unfortunate events that allowed this accident to come to pass." It spoke of the "sadness that permeated the girders of the Towers," of the "on-going investigation into the circumstances surrounding the President's demise" that were being conducted "in public and private chambers throughout the University and State." "Rumors" had "surfaced" in the "region of the ice mountains" and elsewhere that "led" the investigators to "infer a web of error" had been "projected" into various "projects in progress" and that this "web" would be "seen to" in the "near future in the hopes that such occurrences of simultaneity and simulation" did not "manifest themselves in the University again."

It spoke of "a time when the University will have to rethink itself and begin again in ways that have heretofore never been seen by eye of beast or man. This time will bring with it a new wind, a new season, not winter, not spring or summer or fall, but a new season, one never before activated. We, the Committee of Committees, are at this moment reformulating old projects, aligning ourselves with proposals the previous administration (may she rest in peace) left unconsidered, left to gather dust, works of possible genius it is our task to uncover. Who knows what insights may lie there! But we do not wish to make too much of this. We will consider those scientists who have spent their careers in and analyzing dust, but we will consider them for only a short time. Certain designs have had to be shifted into areas once scheduled for 'potential debilitation.' All funds, when not frozen, have gone into the account of the Committee for the Conservation of Function, who, we feel strongly, will know what to do with them. The making of new by-laws, since the sad event of the President's demise, has occupied much of the Committee's time. By-laws previously considered useful will be looked at once again in a new light, on a new day, through lenses supplied by the Dean of Alterity and his appointees. An orderly transfer—though we wish we did not have to say this—which we expected to appear on the horizon like a gentle colossus, a bound giant buzzed about by flies on a dusty road, has brought with it instead clouds of a nature that belie any orderliness and which we currently have under advisement. *Ein Fremdarbeiter*, or worker from the outerlands, is being questioned regarding the events surrounding the demise of the President. 'Information is forthcoming, always,' as she used to like to say, a statement we, too, support whole-heartedly. Sometimes we are afraid, let us be the first to admit. It has yet to be established whether AE [the Artificial Eye] will give the H-P [Head-in-Progress] memory or not. Three-dimensional structural folding has been suggested, and this is under advisement. We are proceeding, even under these difficult circumstances. There is nothing else for us to do but make the best of it. An awful thing has happened to the University, but the University will see its way through. H Tower and S Tower, with only a few glitches, for which we apologize in advance, hum on. Certain cells of the body will always play tricks. We have these under advisement. This is the end of the report as it now stands. *Vielen Dank*."

On the third day they came into my cell and asked me if I would write a report, it needn't be more than two thousand words, on the Official Report, but I refused to oblige them.

That I can't do, I said.

Why not, they asked.

Because the Official Report is pure fiction, and fiction, as the President once told me, should be passed over, if at all, in silence.

Then you refuse?

I see no point in not refusing.

All you have to do is give us your own personal, no matter how idiosyncratic, notions regarding the Official Report. Is that asking too much? A few statements on the nature of TOR, a few simple but well chosen words on OFF. Won't you do this for us, Herr Abjectus, won't you help the Committee? Surely you have an opinion or two regarding what you have read; surely even you can manage this.

Of course I had an opinion, and of course I could, if I so desired, do as they asked. "The Official Report, i.e., the Preliminary Report on the Assassination of the President," in which the word "assassination" was never, after its first mention, mentioned again, I found about 99% obfuscation. But it was that remaining percent which mystified me into silence.

I have nothing more to add to what I've already told you about the assassination of the President, and nothing to say about TOR or OFF, this packet of fancy you call official.

But what if we made you an offer?

Such as?

They huddled together, their heads nodding like magpies, then unhuddled and said, We will take that under advisement.

They left me, then, these strange figures from the Committee of Committees (or perhaps they were only a subcommittee of the Committee; in retrospect I am sure of this, if nothing more), bowed out of my cell, their robes crackling on the cold floor as they went.

On the fourth day they let me out of my windowless cell and allowed me to wander the corridors of H Tower, but I was not allowed into my cubicle on 9a nor was I allowed to leave the building. The corridors no longer were the corridors I once walked. I, the President's personal assistant, once upon a time walked, no, strode from one Presidential request to another. Nor were they the hives of deceit and subtlety they had become in the weeks before the President's death, where every inch of the floors seemed honeycombed with conspiratorial possibility. Now they were only corridors at any university. Students muddled in and out of the classrooms; professors carried books and papers, chemistry sets and astrolabes, briefcases and tuning forks, in their arms; and the deans fluttered darkly up and down the floors.

Each day my interrogators would come back and ask me again if I would write a report on the Official Report, only a few words, that is all we ask, and each day I disobliged them.

On the fifth day they asked, Will you, Herr

Abjcectus, write a report on the Official Report?

No.

On the sixth day they asked, Will you give us your impressions of OFF?

No.

On the seventh day they shut off the heat, and I began writing.

26. Rumors (II)

After I turned in my report on the Official Report ("I, Herr Thomas Abjectus, personal assistant to the late Ihre Magnifizenz, hereby state that I have read the fiction acronymed TOR and can state that no word in it has a referent in reality"), the Committee of Committees asked me if I would supply to the Committee within one (1) week a report that explained why I am the way I am. I said, What's the offer? They said, Free passage out of the State, if not the country, and severance pay. The figure they presented was, by my or most anyone's standards, a tidy sum. I said, Okay, and they released me.

But even in my attic room during the week I worked on the penultimate report, rumors—whisperings and inclinations inflected with innuendo and misgivings—swirled up to me, as I lay on my pallet and stared at the low gray sky or at the ethereal mountains in my Friedrich print and listened to the thunder roll in over the mountains, foreboding more winter, more ice and snow.

In my grocery store on Urbanstrasse, Yolcu Serinyol Lebensmittel und Schnellimbiss, I heard rumors about the President's demise that said it was only a dismissal. In the *Stuttgarter Nachrichten* the rumors bored like woodlice into the newsprint. Even in my bank, where I went to see if my severance pay had been deposited, the clerks whispered to one another as I passed their stalls, whispers that were swallowed up by the wind when I went out onto the street and peered into the thickly falling snow.

The wind came from all directions, "according to strange and remote behests which one could never guess at," as I read in an ancient text long ago, and only now recalled as I made my way through the alleys heavy with snow back to my attic room, where I would begin the process of sifting fact from rumor, rumor from fact, fact from legend, legend from rumor.

I heard it said that Dunkelbach was a foreigner hired years ago to teach obscure works such as *The Incubator Man, The War of the Sexes, Tyrant and Slave-Girl on Planet Venus, Haunted Atoms, The Great Snow, Into Plutonian Depths, The Girl with the Hungry Eyes, Amorous Philandre, The Lurking Fear, The Arrhenius Horror, Black Thirst, A Man, a Maid, and Saturn's Temptation, Queen of the Black Coast, The Man from the Moon, The Fox Woman, The Face in the Abyss.*

Dunkelbach, it is true, had developed a (derivative) system of the fantastic that gave him some renown, within the limited circles of academe, but because of his being from a different country (?), he could never rise above a C3 position, condemned in the hell of C3 forever. But in no way did he have the renown, both within the University and abroad, the publications and fans, followers and slaverers, from the student body that this rumor professed him to have. This "foreign" Dunkelbach was an assassin sub-contracted by the government from a subcontractor of Dunkelbach's government, and, having now ful-filled his contract, was living in Halifax for the next six months to do research on his forthcoming (and handsomely advanced) *Das Traumgebilde und der Wachtraum* (The Dream Creation and the Waking Dream).

I heard it said that Dunkelbach was a dean in disguise—the Dean of Perpetuity, the Dean of Dance, the Dean of Persona and Development, the Dean of Rewards and Remittance, the Dean of Dismissal—hired by a special committee to investigate, but not assassinate—no, not at all—the President, and that this rumor about Dunkelbach having assassinated her had no validity. He was, at best, an innocent by-stander, though proof was available, proof was locked away from the public's eyes to be revealed only when needed, proof awaited in the wings that Dunkelbach was, at the time of the President's collapse, delivering a paper entitled "Re-gendering Norhala: Goddess of the Inexplicable" at a conference on science fiction in Timișoara.

But in all of the rumors, even the most mun-dane, fancy bested fact, reality was consistently ig-nored.[**] For example, in one, everything had occurred

[**]I would like to note here that also odd was the fact that none of the ru-mors—some of which faded as quickly from memory as a dream dreamt at that last moment between sleep and wake, others which lingered long enough to become legend, and for the legend to solidify into monuments

149

just as it had happened, except instead of a gun shot, there was only an astonished look on the President's face as she clutched her left breast and died on the spot of a coronary thrombosis.

One day, as I stepped off the 42 bus onto Landhausstraße, I heard someone behind me say, *Ihre Magnifizenz ist nicht tot. Sie ist ein Bahnhof*—or at least that's what I thought I heard ("Her Magnificence isn't dead, she's a train station"?), I can't be sure. When I turned around, I saw only a collage of huge-lipped, low-browed, overweight Swabian housewives and mail carriers, as if I were looking into a painting by Breughel the Elder, and amongst these faces, none showed any interest in me. Later that night, as I drifted off, I wondered if it were possible that the President in fact had not died, that the person killed had been a double, a player hired to do a job and in her final performance decided not even then to step out of character. Or was this only delusion on my part, only a last sorrowful hope of not losing my President forever?

(black obelisks, usually) set at the end of the Towers' corridors to commemorate this heroic act (Dunkelbach leaning over the President, listening to her dying words while hoping still she could be saved) or that dread deed (above one obelisk hung a painting—"The Fleeing Few"—of a ship in a storm, empty of all crew except a single, drenched Mus musculus domesticus)—bore the slightest resemblance to the (empty and evasive) Official Report. Information, by the way, continues to flood in, information that demands immediate updating, and I am busy processing it even as I write. Thus thoroughness and completeness has not been absolutely and to the letter of the contract fulfilled. All of this put beside the immensity of character and will that was the President as I knew her (though I admit, yes, that I had begun to have my doubts, even then, yes, even then, regarding the benignity of the President's every action, but she did tell me, didn't she, that I am too susceptible), put beside the complexity of Ihre Magnifizenz, my report is but a trope made of ropes knotted for someone else to undo.

Who can mark the line where violet ends and orange begins? One moment my heart passionately yearned for the President to still be alive, as passionately as one imaginative heart can, and I wanted desperately to believe the fact that somewhere in all these legends, some truth lay. But the next moment I knew she was gone, that the legend of her continuance was a lie, a story told to make someone feel more secure within the limits of their (small or not) epistemological space. For myself, I allowed only that perhaps she had fled her pain, and was now no longer of this earth, asleep in oblivion's arms.

Nonetheless, there was, it seems, no end to the rumors. The President and the Head-in-Progress, it was said, were always one, but that when the President died, so did the H-P and the AE and G-Chamber—all her favorite and most secret projects!—and that the Head had transformed first into a spider, a very small spider, and that this spider had attached itself to the face of a *Volksmädchen*, a young woman with milk bucket in hand, and that her cheek then blossomed black as a cloud, and from this cloud had issued a host of spiders who ravaged the countryside and the people, or, variously, that the Head, now that the President was dead, had nothing more to say, merely sat there day after day in its vast chamber, no thought processes able to be recorded any longer, the men frozen on their ladders with paint buckets of medicine in hand, unsure how to revive it. But I recognized these rumors as the literary fancies of the Dean of Dramaturgy and Dislocation, full of Gotthelfian horror with touches of Kafka's famous "*Die Verwandlung*" (Death of a

Salesman) and Chamisso's *Peter Schlemihls wunders-ame Geschichte* (The Man Who Sold His Shadow).

One rumor, perhaps the most fantastic of all (ALL) the rumors, had me (subservient, not subversive, obsequious in many eyes, charity case of a personal assistant, me—ME, of all the infinitude of possibilities!) sitting in Dunkelbach's office, at Dunkelbach's desk, reading Dunkelbach's three folders without his consent, and becoming so inspired by what I read, that after nodding to my fanatical figure in the mirror I rushed into an elevator, hopped off on the eleventh floor, brushed brutally past the game but lame and screaming secretary, tumbled over the threshold of the President's inner chambers, righted myself at once, and shot the astonished woman, steaming tea cup in hand, dead.

And there was that vicious, sickest of rumors I heard one afternoon in the middle of the week at the newsstand on Schlossplatz, that foulest traduction, that said she, Ihre Magnifizenz, had never been President, had never been Ihre Magnifizenz, that she was only a demon-haunted soul, an absence, a force of negation, and that Dunkelbach, in having rid us of this negation, was our savior.

But how, I wondered as I wrote "Why I Am the Way I Am" for the Committee, how could the woman I had known, the President, Ihre Magnifizenz, in her ordinary splendor, in her splendid ordinariness, be a demon of any kind, be in any way connected to these fairy tales? Other fairy tales, yes—of a child lost in the snow, of a snowstorm entrapping two children one Christmas eve atop a mountain, of a winter storm obliterating memory—but not to any I heard.

Throughout the week, while the rumors and legends and their attendant questions, like midges in a country lane swirling up into your face, distracted me even in my dreams, I worked laboriously and with increasing dissatisfaction on my report.

Finally, at week's end, not at all pleased with the result, I threw away what I had written and penned instead a childhood memory. I had no idea (*Ich habe keine Ahnung*—my first words in German) what the Committee would think of it, but in my despair I was beyond caring.

27. Why I Am the Way I Am

WHY I AM THE WAY I AM

I would like to preface my remarks here with a brief statement of gratitude for the time I have been allowed to work at this university which was granted to me by one and only one person, i.e., the late Ihre Magnifizenz. If not for this singular, not altogether short, woman, this powerful figure who overcame so much dissension and strife and yet managed to run the University with such diplomatic, political, and administrative legerdemain, I would never have been spirited away from my life of pumping gas at Chet Darling's Downtown Mobil and cleaning out the ice house (my favorite activity on dry, summer afternoons) and sipping a coke while sitting next to the crank-handled cola machine and perusing a book or two—, would never, that is, been given the opportunity to escape this Arkansas idyll my grandmother rightfully taught me to disdain, as if it were so much detritus, so much kitsch.

Next, let me say that this is an assignment that does not come easily to me. I prefer, when I write, to write for someone else, as I used to do for the President. I do not like writing about myself. That said, I have endeavored here to relate to you events that occurred on the single most important day of my life, the day that most helped to form, as best as I can assess, the character I am today.

(The second-most important day, i.e., the day I was hired by the President, I believe the Committee is already sufficiently cognizant of, and thus will not be alluded to in this report.)

In M___, a small town of no importance in southern Arkansas, my grandmother, Madame O___, a widow of unsullied reputation and mother of my mother, stepped out of the door of the wood frame house she was visiting and where my parents and I lived on the outskirts of M___, and shouted to me at play in the field on the other side of the road. "Abse, come home! Look at those clouds! A storm's coming."

Intent on my game of following a carpenter ant for the past hour as it weaved its way through the weeds carrying a crumb of white bread four times its size, I had not noticed the sky beginning to roil with clouds so dark they looked bruised. I gathered my empty pail, my toy shovel, and aggie marble (an obstacle for the ant to skitter over), and ran back across the road to my grandmother.

For some time we stood together, her hand resting firmly on my shoulder, and stared into the blue-black, bedeviled sky, and saw there seven tornadoes, like strange monsters dropped from a dark womb, twist down from a cloud, hold there for a moment, then sway slightly as if deciding the direction it wanted to turn, then, like the beak of some fantastic bird, swoop down and peck the earth—once, twice—then bounce back up into the sky. And each time the tornado touched down, my grandmother and I said, "Ah, ah, let's hope no one was hurt."

Though we could see them in the distance, the tornadoes were still at least an hour away from us, and there was little we could do in preparation—the nearest storm cellar was ten miles away and my parents had taken our old Dodge into town to see *Winter Meeting* starring Bette Davis (my mother's favorite actress) at the Cameo. We knew the routine, my grandmother and I: go to the center of the house, into a room with no windows if possible (not for us), cover up your head, and pray. Until that time, it was best to observe the weather. It's possible, if you see one coming soon enough, to outrun or side-step a tornado, though my grandmother didn't really believe we could do that.

After a while, I drifted away from her toward the ditch beside the road and began to look for polliwogs or spring peepers in the water, or more carpenter ants or doodle bugs in the dirt, or grasshoppers or crickets—any of the numerous small creatures that made the ditch a haven for me to drift into and talk to them as if they could understand me, and dream for hours. Today though, with the wind pulling the leaves off the cottonwood (the only tree in our front yard which was mostly dirt except for a scraggly forsythia and a few strands of struggling grass) and the air charged with storm, I could see nothing aswim in the dank water or crawling in the ditch. I dug a little in the dirt trying to uncover an earthworm or beetle, but even these seemed to be in hiding from the impending storm.

Finally, at the exact moment I thought I had spied a peeper poke its eyes from behind a leaf in the shallow, muddy water, a strange sound rang out to me: "Caw caw! Caw caw!"

I crawled out of the ditch on my hands and knees, smudging my bare kneecaps, and saw two black crows standing in the road with their beaks open and their eyes staring as if in amazement at me.

I spread my arms and stared down at my tattered and mud-splattered t-shirt and shorts, expecting to find a chafer or tiger beetle on my chest, but nothing was there.

Then both crows flew at me, and I flung my arms over my face.

"Wha?" I cried, dodging these black missiles as they flew past me. "Wha!"

I fell back into the ditch, started to cry

louder, until my grandmother came running out to me.

"Git, you old birds!" she screamed at the crows.

Startled, they hopped back to the road.

"Shame on you both," she said to them, and they cawed back to her. "Now get out of here, you devils, before I come after you."

They flapped away back up the road and quickly vanished from view.

My grandmother bent down to the wailing urchin beside her and lifted him into her arms. With a child's passion I clutched her bosom, pushed my face deep into her right breast, and sobbed, "Why did they attack me?"

She carried me in her arms onto the porch where we sat on the steps—the air crackling cold against our bare forearms, the clouds, like giants in combat, thundering dark blue above us.

"Well, Abse," she said, "that's a difficult one, let me tell you. But I'll give it a try. You see, crows can fly, but can't sing very well, and they feel insulted when they see a poor child happier than they. Here at the bottom, Abse, the dogs fight over scraps. It's possible that the crows understand this. I remember a story that my grandmother told me, and you yourself may someday wish to tell your grandchildren. Friends of my great-grandfather Georg tell me it's an old Germanic tale; others, friends of my great-grandmother Mimmie, tell me that it's a Choctaw legend. Its goes like this—

"Once upon a time a poor child lost his mother and father, and then everything on the earth withered and died, and there was no one anymore for the child to play with. Everything was dead, and all day and all night the child cried. And because there was no one any longer on the earth, the child wished she could live in the sky, where the moon gazed down so friendly. Then it descended and the child put its finger on the moon, but the moon was only a rancid piece of cheese. And then the sun came down to the child, but when the child put out its hand to take in its friendliness and warmth, the sun was only a rotted sunflower. Then it was the stars' turn, but when the child looked at that first star it had placed so many wishes upon, it was a tiny, golden maggot that had crawled out of the corpse of the child's mother, and the second star was a carrion beetle that had crawled out of the runny eye of the child's father. The child wished the earth itself would crumble like ash in a wind, and the earth obliged it. Then the child sat down on the nothingness beneath it and cried and cried, and there it sits still and is totally alone."

Pondering this tale, I soon forgot about the crows that had attacked me. We sat together another hour, watching the storm clouds turn away from us, as if they had suddenly lost all interest in us, as if we were now unworthy of them, or at best irrelevant.

Then it grew dark and colder still, and my grandmother and I went back inside.

28. A Short, but Annoying, Colloquy

For some reason, they did not respond to my "self-analysis" other than to acknowledge its receipt (via late night messenger—the long walk down the stairs to the ground floor from my attic room; the messenger, little taller than a meter, in his heavy coat covered with light-gray tufts of hair from an animal I could not identify, swaying in front of me with a form I had to sign that kept fading into the snow and reappearing out of it) and to let me know that my severance pay and money for a ticket out of the State, the region, the land, was now being transferred into my account. The message went on to say that my "office" on 9aHT was available for my temporary use until the middle of the week.

Meanwhile, rumors about the death of the President swirled through the corridors and offices of the University. After she was shot—and she was, I saw Professor Dunkelbach do it, even if no one believes me—Russian scientists hijacked her soul into cyberspace where it was being used to help install

"Tower" projects abroad. Or: The President's body rested comfortably, albeit vegetal, on a man-made atoll, where quantum physicists from every country were convened to study it. Or: She had been stabbed, poisoned, filleted by A, B, C, or D. A daughter, long unknown, would soon appear and proclaim her ascendancy to the throne. Preparations were underway, but for what no one could say. The Head-in-Progress and the Activated Eye, two of her administration's most important projects, had been deactivated. New elections would be announced soon; the late President was barred from running. The President wasn't really the President, that is, she was the President, but she wasn't real; she was a jewel who possessed the thought patterns of the President, and this jewel resided at the base of the President's skull, that is, the body that represented the President. The jewel did not know that it did not know that it did not know that it did not know that it was the President; to all intents and purposes it was the President, so when the President was shot, it felt: I have been shot. Now I must die. But it did not die. It lived on. It lives on still. It is in contact with the natives of planet Lithia, through ESP. The natives of Lithia have flowers for heads and the bodies of reptiles. Giant lepidoptera flutter in and out of Lithian homes. The jewel is in contact with them. The University monitors their communications.

And what was my role, now that my President was dead? Once the President's personal assistant, I sifted and sorted this mostly worthless nonsense, while I made plans to leave the city. Why did I expect to discover in the nonsense a grain of sense? Perhaps I simply wanted no longer to worry about the intrigues of the University, of the loss I felt whenever the word "President" came to my mind or ear. I also avoided going back to the Towers, Humanities or Sciences. I did not want to run into any of my soon-to-be former colleagues.

But finally I had packed up my attic room—the paperbacks, the Friedrich print—and there was nothing left for me to do but go back to my cubicle.

On the next morning before I went to the University, as I sat over a cup of tea and a croissant at KönigX, I noticed advertised in the *Stuttgarter Zeitung* a roman à clef by Robert Rohrzerspringer, due within the month from Kuhschellen Verlag, München. The advertisement took up only a quarter of an inch of the bottom of page 27, but I could see, faintly, a photo of the author—his moustache, his smile—or perhaps I was only imagining it, the picture was so small I became lost in the dots and spaces. But the words beneath it, a blurb by one H. Dunkelbach, the Universität, Institut für Literaturwissenschaft Amerikanistik, were as clear and concise as they were empty and bloated to my confused, astonished eyes:

Rohrzerspringer's masterpiece! *Die Universität* is a tale of high political intrigue, a study in the effects of power on a President, as narrated by her personal assistant, at a strange university, known eponymously as the Universität, somewhere in southern Germany. It's a fantasy extravaganza of academe, a science fiction love story Merrittean in its achievement and goals, an epistemological meditation, a heady brew of baseness and belliger-ence, the metaphysical and the mundane, and, not insignificantly, a heartfelt quest from first word to last. Within the walls of the Universität, the reader will encounter such oddities of imagination and design as the Barn-in-Progress and the Activated Chamber and the Gestating Eye and a wonderland of bizarre, earth-tilting dreams. All this, yet there's more! Danger and fear swirl around the President and her loyal aide as they try to discover who or what is behind the rumors of subversive deans plotting an overthrow of the Universität, or worse. Suspense at every imbedded turn! It's a romp, a riot, a gay escapade of the wildest imagination, and a true and serious and caring insider's look at the machinations of academe. In sum: Rohrzerspringer's masterpiece, nothing more nor less, and penned with a heart and mind and grasp worthy of a Tomzack or Rübezahl.

How quickly they (THEY) worked! I thought, and flung the paper down, rattling the spoon in my saucer. Obviously others were enough in the know to know how both to reveal and obfuscate the truth. Obviously others had access to my and the President's files, and when I arrived at my cubicle there would be nothing left. Obviously someone was willing (and eager) to profit from the misery of others (my and the President's). Obviously someone had scrawled over the page of truth a pack of disingenuous distortions and lies. And most obviously, most obviously, one Professor Dunkelbach was somehow behind it all!

I rushed to H Tower, but instead of going up to 9a, stopped off on 4a, where I banged on Dunkelbach's door with my fist. No one answered. I banged my copy of the *Stuttgarter Zeitung* on the door. No one answered. I banged with both fist and paper and shouted, Dunkelbach, are you in there? No one answered. Then someone did.

A woman in her late twenties opened the door and said, in a voice both haughty and haunting, May I help you? She wore jeans and an ash-gray turtleneck and held in one hand a cup of coffee and in the other a tattered copy of A. Merritt's *Dwellers in the Mirage*. Her face was oval, the exact oval of the wire frames of her glasses, her nose small but well-formed. With her right (book) hand, she swept her short nut-brown hair off her forehead.

Where's Dunkelbach, I asked.

Not here, she said, and turned sideways for me to look past her face and sweatered breasts into Dunkelbach's office. I took a step forward, stood on my tiptoes, and saw that Dunkelbach wasn't there.

What can I do for you? she asked.

And then began the following short but annoying colloquy:

Who are you?

Who are you?

The Pres..., the late President's assistant.

And I'm Herr Dunkelbach's student assistant. Pleased to meet you, as they say in your country.

I thought C3s weren't allowed assistants.

He's not a C3; he's only a Lektor.

I thought Lektors didn't get assistants either.

They don't.

But...

I'm paid out of private funds.

I see. Could you tell me where I can find Dr. Dunkelbach?

You haven't heard?

About what?

His wife fell seriously ill, acute depression, three months ago. He's been there all winter.

I see. Three months ago, you say?

Yes.

When does he return?

He doesn't know. But he calls me every night. If you want to leave a message, I can pass it along.

No thanks.

A pleasure meeting you.

She thrust the hand with the book in it for me to shake, which I did not (had she expected me to take the damn thing?), then shut the door.

I took the elevator (achingly, yawningly, slow in coming) to 9a.

I opened the door to my cubicle. As I thought, my file cabinets were empty, my desk in shambles.

When I bent down to start picking up what the conspirators had thrown to the floor, I noticed something flutter in the closet door mirror.

I stood up and looked again.

Within the mirror, the President smiled and vanished.

29. Life

And then reappeared again in the mirror, stepped out of it, and walked toward me, wearing her broad, pleasant smile and her charcoal-gray suit with three delicate gold necklaces over her white silk blouse.

Ihre Magnifizenz!

Well, said the figure, as it passed through me, causing a tingling in my blood, not quite, Herr Außenseiter, not quite.

She sat down on my desk, raised a skirted knee into her clasped hands, and offered me her broad, generous smile.

I see, she said, gazing around the wrecked room, that you've been too long alone. That's snow, yes, you see on my black buckle shoes. And why are you still working overtime? Best take care of yourself, Herr Abjectus, if you want ever to work again.

I nodded to the ghost on my desk, but I was too astonished at what was happening to confess to any understanding of what she had said.

Yes, Thomas, I am dead but still with you, still with you but dead. So much to think about, so much still to resolve. No one individual, no single human being, and so on. What did they expect I would do if they succeeded in ousting me? Play dead? How little they know me! My little assistant, when realities are melting from me, I am at my strongest. Surely you have not forgotten that.

Outside, beyond the well-dressed figure (a double? but how could she have passed through my body?), I could see dusk settling on the edges of the valley, and the wind whipped crows and magpies from a birch tree.

What was she trying to tell me? Was she really there on my desk? What was happening?

But instead of an answer, the President simply rocked for a moment with her knee still held in her hands and smiled down on me.

What would they think of me, if I were to return? But it really doesn't matter, does it? Oh, were you sorrowful, were you disturbed, were you dismissed for misconduct, for standing up for me? I'm so grateful, but it wasn't necessary. It's all due to this long winter, isn't it? One would think we weren't at all concerned about the fate of our students. But that is not true, not at all the case. What is the case is that matters must be continued in a fashion commensurate with the developmental potential of the cognitive skills of the students so that some day they might match the cognitive skills of the Ministries of Finance and Devotion, Education and Vibrant Emptying, and then, you see, we will have the fortitude and wisdom to behave in a manner befitting a public institution which exists at the behest of the Ministry of Mysterium and the State.

Think about it, Thomas. These are strange times. Why don't we make the most of them, you and I? What do you say? Are you with me once again? That ride through the forests of Arkansas after I plucked you from your work at Chet Darling's Downtown Mobil in Fordyce and made you my personal assistant. Were those eagles or crows in the sky? Are there eagles in Arkansas? An old black man came up to me and said he had been reading the Book of Revelations and that if I touched him I would be blessed. Is that true? The day was fair, not a cloud in the sky, and my mind was as empty as a Norwegian shadow.

The clouds outside the Towers had sunk lower, their foreheads grown heavier, and the room darkened around us.

Thomas, the President continued, I have always admired your reports, even if I did not have time to read them all. I found your style a quiet kind of stroll, not at all obtrusive. You learned to let the words lead down corridors even I did not know existed. And you know, don't you, that you have one final report to file. Listen to them, Herr Abjectus. Can you hear them? Right now the deans are debating on the senate floor about funding the Gestation Chamber. They don't know where the monies for that project came from. But I do. Listen to them, Thomas. Can't you hear them? As brash as blue jays. Listen to them. Gaps, they say. Cracks, crevices, fissures. A dialectical misunderstanding, they say. First we must frame the zone, they say. Then the notion of a frame for the President will have to be renegotiated in committee. Whoever can bite their noses, Herr Thomas, as I often say. Can you see them? What strange figures they are in their robes and masks, old buzzards around the carcasses of their desks. Official histories pour out of their mouths, and fantasies from their presses. But don't they know what is about to happen to them? Do they have to be dragged to the truth like a dog to a bath? What is wrong with them?

I don't know, Ihre Magnifizenz, I offered, but in a voice so low I do not think she heard me.

I must live, Herr Thomas, she said. I must. The snow and the moon know that. It's endless, the history of the world. How can we step through the endlessness to find the *Sein* within the *Dasein*? That, you see, is why I've come back.

She paused for a moment, raised her right hand, and passed her forefinger back and forth in front of her lips. Her eyes closed, and she seemed to be resting, or perhaps she was pondering her next thought, her next word.

And, she said, hasn't this always been my goal? I have my allies, who are as determined as I. Shall I mention a single name? The Minister of Mysterium. That's right, Thomas, an old friend. I've heard stories are told about us. We go back a long way, too long, some say. Contingencies, I said, must precede the Plan, and the doors to the Ministerium spread wide.

She ruffled her charcoal jacket, swept her dark hair (more mussed than usual today) from her face, and let out a long, eerie (because, after all, she was, as far as I knew, dead), and voluminous laugh into the small chamber. I saw (or thought I saw) the ghostly gray air stir around her.

Remind me, Herr Abjectus, to tell you about the fate of your predecessor. Much can be learned from the mistakes of others, and from one's own. Yes, I, too, have erred. I, too, have stood in front of the Hauptbahnhof and not understood the master's words. Doubt crawls over us like vermin, eating us, devouring us, sticking in our throats until we can't speak, can't breathe. Dear Thomas, glory partakes of no doubts. One cannot found a new university on such a basis. One needs vision, cash, and patience. O my soul longs for an institution worthy of my music! But I do not despair, Thomas, anymore than should you.

She came toward me then and held out her hands. Slowly I raised my own to this magnificent figure, before whom I trembled in awe. And when our fingers touched, a tingle went through me comparable only to certain rare moments in music when one note or chord lifts another with such delicacy and care that of a sudden you feel the energy radiating from the great Yggdrasil which covers the universe with knowledge and light.

Though she still stood before me, my hands held lightly by her fingertips, Ihre Magnifizenz seemed to sweep down upon me as if from on high, her lips brushing lightly my cheek, her words whispering in my ear.

What you are about to see has never been revealed to anyone before, and you must tell no one of this dream, which after a time is all it will seem. Do you accept the story I've told you so far?

Completely, I said, her lips feathering my ear when I nodded.

Then listen further. The less thought, the more grace, as the old puppeteer had it. As with lines in infinity, you must someday meet yourself either coming or going, and when you do, you must then make the crossover. This is what I have done. The hollow mirror before the mirror can reflect only itself, but only then can it be contained. Whoever enters infinity returns with grace. But who can do that? Can the deans? Can the students? Can you? Can the University be a part of teaching us how? That was where my administration, when abruptly cancelled, was headed. From that peak I planned to lead the other universities throughout the State, the country, and perhaps push on even farther, to the edges of the frontier and beyond. Do they think now I cannot? Elsewhere, too, there are winds to be studied. Elsewhere, too, it is snowing. Do the deans know how to stop it? They don't even realize its extent. This is why I had to fire the Dean of Weather, the Provost of Storms. They understood nothing of the metaphysics of snow; they never understood where it could take us. Do you? Can you? Can you puzzle it out, this old European system that has tangled us so long? Can you escape before the Towers turn on their axes and take wing to the north or east? I have one more thing to show you, Thomas, and then you can decide whether or not you will follow me on the journey into the mirror before the mirror. The question for you is: What will I return as, a marionette or a god?

And then she wrapped her arms around me, and they grew longer and longer, I felt a feather fluttering against my closed eyelids, felt her neck elongate beneath my clutching hands, and then we were in the air, but I did not open my eyes. I did not want ever to be as afraid as I was once before aloft on the back of the President. I refused to open my tightly closed eyes, and prayed fervently, as I clung to her neck, that when we landed, I would awake to find myself at the window looking out onto S Tower at the President at her window looking back at me.

But when I opened my eyes, we were in an enormous room standing before a huge wooden vat, as big as the Heidelberg Tun, with wires and pipes and tubes and rubber hoses and cables pumping liquid energy into a glowing, roiling stew.

The Gestation Chamber, the President said.

It looked like... what? Like a giant's watch built inside out by a madman, like a carnival going up (or coming down?), like the cypress-shrouded snake pond in the Cooter Neck woods near which I grew up after my parents' death. It looked something like all those things, and it looked nothing like them. It chugged and gurgled and burbled and smelled a little like burnt toast and a little like the wind in an ice storm, knife-sharp and clean.

The President took me by the hand and led me up to the strange thing, and then she placed my palm on its weathered, warm wood.

Always my favorite project, Herr Gehülfe, always where I funnelled the discretionary funds. From here the University will grow a third arm, a fourth Tower, a fifth Eye. From here the University will become the Milky Way University, University U. Around the world I will hold a conference on the Wings of Misery, on Dirigibles and their Place in Education Today. We will meet in hotels, in resorts, in ships, in senates. Bids from China have far exceeded those from Russia. We will build a Tower in Beijing, and one in Roanoke, Virginia, and one on Lake Thun. And you can be with me, dear Thomas, or you can be alone again. I cannot help you decide, except to say that within the Gestation Chamber a maelstrom awaits unlike any you've known before. For a while you float in the margins in sight of it, but then suddenly are pulled into the clashing of its great liquid walls. Here, at the black center, in the navel of the vortex, the white seed of gestation is ignited, and you will arise again, Thomas, no longer a marionette, and bob on the waves of life for days, for years, perhaps for centuries.

The President placed her hands on my shoulders, and I stared for the last time into her alert, bright, welcoming eyes—, but I did not fall into them. I was too afraid.

She smiled, and from her lips, as her fingers left my arms, a radiant light briefly broke forth. Then quickly she turned away, stepped toward the Gestation Vat, and vanished.

30. Conclusions

I have packed and nothing of me remains within the University except my reports, which are already sifting through the system, contaminating a strange cabinet here, a stray chip there. I leave as well this final report, as requested by the Committee, whom I wish to thank for giving me the opportunity to present my case in a manner I thought only befitting, considering the peculiar nature of my work in this institution. I trust I can be trusted. I trust you believe my words. But if you don't, then that's your loss, not mine. I am going away. Where am I going? I am going away.

Conclusions are difficult to come by. If this were about conclusions, I would have given up long ago. My tenure has been a stimulating, if sorrowful, one. I take with me secrets I cannot even reveal to myself.

Did Dunkelbach escape punishment? Was it the President or her double he tried to kill? Why did the Committee show no interest in my first report written directly for them? Did I dream the scene in the Gestation Chamber, or did it dream me?

I can't say, *ich weiß nicht, je ne sais pas, nescio, j'ai*

174

pas, ich habe keine Ahnung, I don't know.

And the President? No, I need say nothing more about her. She's spoken well enough for herself, I think.

But there is one thing more I remember that she told me, one last thing which might be of interest to the Committee. But on second thought, it might not. At any rate, and for what it's worth, she told me, on our first meeting, as she ran her forefinger across my cheek, *Die Unsterblichkeit paßt Ihnen* (Immortality becomes you)—a compliment I could hardly accept.

Concerning the reports not included in this report, such as the Boxed Head, the Straw Camel, and the Infinite Mouse—these, I believe, are readily available elsewhere (and already being cannibalized!).

This, then, is all I have to report on the President in Her Towers and what I learned therein.

TOM WHALEN is a novelist, short story writer, poet, and critic who has written for *Agni, Bookforum, Film Quarterly, The Iowa Review, Missouri Review,* the *Washington Post* and other publications. Co-editor of the Robert Walser Number of *The Review of Contemporary Fiction*, he has translated and written extensively on Walser's work. He teaches film at the State Academy of Art and Design in Stuttgart, Germany, and literature at various universities.

ellipsis
• • •
press

1. Fog & Car by Eugene Lim

2. Waste by Eugene Marten

3. The Mothering Coven by Joanna Ruocco

4. Shadowplay by Norman Lock

5. The Harp & Altar Anthology, edited by Keith
Newton & Eugene Lim

6. Changing the Subject by Stephen-Paul Martin

7. The Dreaming Girl by Roberta Allen

8. The President in Her Towers by Tom Whalen